Kasumi and the Alien

Dakota Kaine

SilkenShadow Press

Chapter 1
Survivor's Guilt
~ * ~ * ~ * ~

Wintry gusts battered the mountain refuge. Their howls carried an endless melody, haunting yet comforting to him.

I've been here too long. Velamar adjusted his moonlit robe and repositioned the candle which burned softly at the desk in his study. The cup of coffee he'd made from the matter-resynthesizer had long since gone cold. He held onto the crystal, purest ivory fissured with veins of color ranging from lapis lazuli to periwinkle. It comforted him, this, his one connection to the outside world. Well, not his *only* connection. Not anymore.

"Are you coming to bed soon?"

There she stood in all her glory. Perhaps 'glory' wouldn't have been the word that most men of his kind would have used. Though she was not of his species, though she was human, he found her no less attractive. In fact, there were still times, quiet, unremarkable moments, when she dazzled him just by her very being.

"Why?" he asked, his voice filled with good humor. "Cold again?"

Kasumi Ogawa tiptoed on her bare feet across the freezing stone floor, wrapped her arms around his shoulders from behind and gave the back of his mottled head a kiss.

"Point of fact, *yes*. I'm *freezing*. Come to bed soon?" When Velamar swiveled in his chair, those pleading eyes dared him to say no. Then, when she bent down to kiss him, he felt all three of his hearts start to throb. She drew away.

"There might be more where that came from if you hurry to bed soon," she said with an arched eyebrow and a smirk. His eyes lingered on her as she walked away, mesmerized by the bob of her jet-black ponytail.

I do not deserve her he thought. Then again, he had not deserved the others either. All of them, his previous companions, had given his life a meaning that was like the very air he needed to draw breath. Each had been unique. Kasumi Ogawa was unique too. But it still saddened him, the selfishness of his good fortune when it came to her.

I'm glad her ship crashed. I'm glad for all of it because it brought her to me. The deaths of 133 people, and I would gladly trade all their lives again if it meant having Kasumi at my side. Did that make him a monster? The thought troubled him, made him lay awake some nights when Kasumi lay soft and warm beside him. It was a truth, a selfish conviction that he never, ever wanted to share with her – perhaps his most shameful secret.

~ * ~

Kasumi slipped back into bed, shimmied under the heavy comforter and stared out the window. The two larger moons and their smaller sibling gleamed as a yellow-white, azure-cream, and pale pink dot surrounded by a halo of distant stars. Qaephar was a cold, desolate planet, and yet life thrived beneath its crust and around geothermal vents. Kasumi felt like one of those tiny organisms, in a way, tucked away in the geothermal vent which was Velamar's home. Now her home too. It still didn't seem that way though. After just over three months, she still felt the ache of loss. Her Captain. Her fellow officers. The rest of the crew. Their faces still rose in her memory, sometimes in her nightmares. She woke up in cold sweats to Velamar's soothing. He knew every detail of her nightmares too. How could he not? He was a powerful telepath.

He had promised her that he would no longer trespass in her thoughts, but she had no way of knowing if it was a promise kept. In fact, she strongly suspected that his care and concern for her overrode any vow to respect her privacy. If it was possible to care *too* much, she felt that Velamar bore that kind of love for her, almost like an obsession. Despite his love, though, she felt lonely sometimes, and not just because her entire crew was dead. Not even because she was stranded on a world dozens of light years away from Earth. She missed her family, her mother and father, her brother, the familiar smells and sights of home – all the things that might comfort someone struggling with monumental loss.

"Kasumi?"

As if he had sensed her melancholy, the alien strode into the bedchamber. He hung up his robe and climbed beneath the covers with her. His body heat instantly suffused her. She took off her nightshirt and cuddled up against him. The sadness in her heart slowly began to melt as his lips kissed their way in a tender path along her brow.

"You're not reading my thoughts, are you?" She tried to look crossly at him but failed, and epically at that.

"I am reading the expression on your face, Kasumi. Some things do not take a mind-reader. You are my companion, my wife. I have already seen and felt all your memories. I know you as if we've been together for a thousand years."

She looked away. She knew *he* knew better. It unsettled her when he spoke like this, but sometimes the alien couldn't help himself. Kasumi decided to take control. Her hands stroked his chest. The oddly colored skin there, the ridges of bone which she'd once regarded as so strange, now seemed attractive to her, their contours sleek and somehow masculine.

"I do not want your pity."

"It is not pity I feel for you, Kasumi. It is simply love. Loyalty. Devotion. Is it wrong for me to have these sacred convictions toward you? Do humans not value these things?"

She put a fingertip to his lips. Kasumi smiled sadly up at him. "No, you're right. Humans do value those things. But sometimes we're afraid. Humans… we don't like to feel vulnerable. That can be a physical feeling, but for us it can be emotional too. We are not as forward as your people are. We hide our emotions. We protect our hearts from the threat of loss." Tears sprang into her eyes. "And right now I would do anything to not keep reliving what happened. To not see my crewmates whenever I close my eyes," she blurted. "Why did I have to be the only one, Vel? Why did I live while they all had to die??"

~ * ~

Because I only had time to save one of you Velamar thought. It was fortunate that *she* could not read minds. He stroked her hair and just tried to soothe her. But after she wiped her eyes, a strength rose up in her. She pressed her cheek into the palm of his four-fingered hand. Kasumi took a shuddery breath, as if drawing mental fortitude from the physical connection they shared.

"I can tell you a story of my people, if it would help. Would you like to hear a story?" he asked softly.

Kasumi shook her head. Her hands slid along his shoulders. "I don't need words right now. I just need *you*." Her meaning was unmistakable, her soft hands gliding along the smoothness of his muscles. Velamar shuddered, his hearts pumping in triumph, the green blood in his veins thundering with need.

"I will do what I can to warm you, my little human."

She grinned at him, wiping away the last of her tears as his bulk blanketed hers, his loving face blotting out the moonlight from the window.

"I expect nothing less," she sighed. Her words drew him in as much as her body, and soon their cares, aches, griefs, and insecurities may as well have yielded to the pull of a black hole far, far away.

~ * ~

Velamar's shaft was not unlike a human male sex organ, except when fully aroused it constantly leaked a whitish-clear fluid that was both designed to arouse the excitement in a female llorien and increase her fertility. Although Kasumi was human, the smell of Velamar's pre-cum had a similar effect, stirring her libido. As he plunged into her, the woman's silken channel hugged against his shaft. He plowed inside her with deep, loving strokes. Her body clung to him. Kasumi buried her face against his shoulder and clung to his back as he pounded into her, joining their bodies as thoroughly as any two bodies had ever been joined. Their interspecies coupling mounted toward the pinnacle of release.

"AH! Kasumi, I love you. I love you so much."

"*Yes*. I love you too, Vel. Fill me. Warm me up," she panted, her hands pressing even harder against the back of his shoulders as if she could cement their bodies closer together with each of his powerful thrusts. Then it happened. Male climax and female pinnacle dovetailed together. Kasumi shuddered as she felt his seed flow through her. The interstellar explorer felt her own pleasure ripple in all directions, her sex convulsing around his life-giving manhood.

At last, the alien sagged on top of her, the smell of sex thick in the air. Velamar's lips swept across Kasumi's brow again, except now it was a brow slick with sweat from their exertions.

"Did that warm up my favorite human?" he murmured.

She giggled beneath him. He was still inside her, slowly softening, but she didn't want him to move. His body heat, the blanket of his form, made her feel safe, and Kasumi's sated body oozed with satisfaction that begged for this moment to last forever. But eventually Velamar rose up on his elbows with a sigh, his manhood slipping free of her slickness. Kasumi gasped, unprepared. She looked down at his still semi-firm cock glistening with their combined fluids, which even now were seeping onto the bed. She frowned, but the frown couldn't last as he bent down to kiss her. Collapsing beside her, he gathered her to him, tucked her head against his chest and told her to sleep.

She did gladly. Sweet exhaustion demanded it. Meanwhile, moonlight and starlight seemed to shine with their approval on the interspecies couple as sleep took them both. For now, there was no loneliness. For now, there was only the comfort of each other's scent and touch.

~ * ~

Chapter 2
Paradise Interrupted
~ * ~ * ~ * ~

The long table in the kitchen nook had a fissured texture not unlike Velamar's Seekstone, its woodsy scent subtle but still present after all these many years. The alien ran his hand over the smooth yet slightly uneven surface. *After living here for over five centuries, even the pieces of furniture feel like they are a part of me* he thought. Today was a difficult day. A sacred day too, though. Anniversaries always were. He checked the display fed in from the weather monitor on the bottom terrace. For once, he wouldn't need to wear a parka.

He stepped out onto the main terrace. Velamar's mountain refuge had six terrace levels, each undergirded by a layer of graded soil fanning out from the side of the mountain. He walked out onto this topmost terrace and strode solemnly over to a line of long, rectangular stone panels in the terrace flooring. These were the deathstones. This was where Velamar's previous four companions were buried. Each stone panel had ornate inscriptions, quotations, and imagery that represented the woman he had loved in life. Velamar regarded the second panel from the right with special reverence today. It was 80 years to the day since his beloved Ilushara had passed.

He read the inscription on her deathstone.

"What you are to me has no ending, and long after my physical body is no more I have just one wish – that you feel my eternal love shining down on you as if from an invisible sun that will never wane, never go supernova, and never die." Velamar smiled. Tears gathered in his eyes. Ilushara loved her sun-metaphors. Of all his past loves, she had been the truest romantic, the one fondest of talking about the eternity of love and their bond together. She had been a rare woman – a bold woman never afraid to take chances. Then again, any woman willing to come live with an exiled hermit on the edge of known space had to be. There were times like this when being nearly immortal seemed like the worst burden a person could ever bear.

More tears gathered and the first teardrops slid down Velamar's mottled cheeks.

~ * ~

A scuffing of boots on stone made Velamar stiffen. Kasumi stepped up beside him. She looped her arm in his.

"You didn't have to come out here," he choked out.

"I wanted to." She said no more. Kasumi felt his grief and knew the inadequacy of simple words. Touch, though, that was another matter. As she leaned against him, she felt like he took strength from it. He still cried, but it was a release of emotion rather than pure grief. It was as if he was saying 'goodbye' to a woman he loved, but also 'hello again' – as if somehow he knew that she was never fully gone.

Perhaps it should have felt weird to Kasumi… knowing that he had had four other true loves before her. Velamar had lived for 552 years and he would probably live for at least two thousand more. He had had wives before her and he would have wives after her. But Kasumi didn't feel jealousy toward those other women. In a strange way, she actually felt gratitude. This man – well technically not 'man' but close enough – had saved her when her ship had crash-landed on his planet, shown love for her, and now she loved him in return. Wanting what was best for Velamar meant above all wanting him not to be lonely. Knowing that these women had helped soothe and assuage that loneliness struck her deeply. If anything, Kasumi regarded them as kindred spirits.

"I'm sorry." She kissed his shoulder before leaning her head against it once more.

"There is nothing for *you* to be sorry for, Kasumi, but I thank you all the same." Then he turned, wiping at his eyes. Then he noticed. He noticed that the petite human standing beside him was wearing nothing more than a tank top and pajama pants.

"Have you lost your mind, woman?"

Kasumi shivered a little and gave him a rueful grin. "Oh, come on. There's no need for scolding. It's 40 degrees Fahrenheit out here. On my homeworld that's regarded as a normal fall day."

Velamar frowned. The alien's ears turned a pronounced red, as they always did when he was in distress.

"The weather on Qaephar is unpredictable. It could plunge to 20 below zero in less than a quarter of the hourglass. Foolish woman, I am taking you inside."

She tried to protest, but Velamar put his arm around her waist and hustled her inside. Once inside, he insisted on grabbing her hands and blowing on them to warm them.

"This is ridiculous. Humans are not that prone to cold!" she protested.

"I well remember fishing your body from the lake," he growled in reply, "and I remember you nearly freezing to death on me too!" he countered.

She cringed at the memory. She had awoken naked in his arms, terrified and disoriented, shivering beside the roaring fire in the fireplace in his study, his body wrapped around hers with eight layers of blankets piled atop them.

It struck her, then, this hyper-concern for her to not be out in the elements, it wasn't just simple care for her. No, he was actually reliving the memory of finding her, of almost not being able to save her. *Why didn't I see it before?* she thought.   —

"OK, I'm sorry. I'm sorry I didn't wear proper winter gear when stepping out onto the terrace, OK?" His face softened, but he still looked stern.   ·

"Can I at least put on a parka and go outside to pay my respects to her?" Kasumi asked. Velamar looked at her dubiously. "Please?"

At last, relenting, he brought Kasumi her parka and helped her put it on. The two of them stepped back onto the main terrace together. They retraced their snowy footprints. Yet just when Kasumi had stepped up to Ilushara's deathstone to bow her head in prayer and pay her respects, the unthinkable appeared. A streak of light fissured the heavens. Their eyes couldn't help but jerk toward it.

There it was, like a fireball hurtling across the sky. Not a fireball though. Not a meteor.

A ship.

~ * ~

Chapter 3
Unwanted Discovery
~ * ~ * ~ * ~

Velamar was already halfway through packing his cold weather and survival gear onto the snow-crawler.

"I'm coming with you," Kasumi insisted, not for the first time. She zipped up her snow pants, fastened her boots, and adjusted her parka.

"No, you are not. It's too dangerous." Velamar tightened the last strap on the first aid pack attached to the back of the crawler, then began to manually open the hangar's portal. Meanwhile, Kasumi was already jumping onto the back of the crawler and putting her hood up.

As the wintry white sky and icy whorls of wind greeted them from outside, Velamar lumbered over and lifted the much smaller woman off of the crawler to set her gently down.

"This is not a debate," he growled.

"The hell it isn't," she fired back. He had leapt onto the crawler now, but she was on his back like a second shadow, her hands slipping and interlocking around his waist.

"I'm coming with you. You may as well accept that and stop wasting time."

He glared at her over his shoulder and spoke to her with barely concealed exasperation, as if he was re-educating a child about something for the sixteenth time. "My physiology is naturally built to withstand extreme cold, Kasumi. Yours is not."

"I'm a communications officer of the Galactic Fleet, Fourth Division, of the Earth Alliance. I may not be 'Mr. Indestructible' like you, but I've completed survival and combat training in a wide array of climates and environments. You may need an extra pair of hands and you damned well know it, especially if we have dozens of injured survivors from that ship. Now stop acting like an overprotective ignoramus and let's get moving."

Velamar adjusted his snow-goggles, looked at her for a long moment. She knew what he was fighting. That same uber-protective urge to keep her safe was rearing its well-intentioned but hideous head. *He still hasn't gotten over almost losing me the day I crashed, so how can I make him see reason?*

"I know these mountains, ravines, cliff-faces, and woods like you know you own body, Kasumi. I have lived here for over five hundred years. If you swear to me that you will do exactly what I say and follow my lead… you may come."

The young woman nodded. "I swear." He stared at her for an eon, sizing her up. Judging. Kasumi knew how excruciating it was for him to even just let her come along. She wasn't about to give him an excuse to leave her behind. Even if he slipped into her thoughts to ascertain her true intentions, he would find the simple truth; she *would* follow his lead. Besides, there was no reason not to. This had been his home long before it had become hers.

Begrudgingly, Velamar started up the crawler. The crawler's hydraulic legs whirred and soon they were rising high above the surface, walking on stilt-like legs of impenetrable zirconen steel. The six legs of the snow-crawler punched through Qaephar's crust like metallic toothpicks spearing through a layer of slightly overcooked cheese. The wind buffeted them. Kasumi clung to Velamar as tightly as physics allowed.

The snow-crawler's task was no simple one either. Deadly hidden crevasses littered much of Qaephar's surface. The sensors in the crawler's two lead feet, before applying full pressure, detected any structural gaps or weaknesses in the tons of snow and ice beneath. They were safe as they traversed their way down the mountain… in theory.

"What happens if the sensors malfunction?" Kasumi shouted. The wind stole away her words, but Velamar's acute hearing caught them anyway.

"Then we find out what happens when I hit the emergency eject button."

He was being flippant on purpose – probably to get back at her for making him let her come. She scowled at him, but between the mask, goggles, and hood pulled up over her head she might as well have been trying to shoot him a telepathic glare.

The next half hour and more felt like at least six times that. The crawler picked a careful path down Fha'Hari Mountain until at last they were in the shelter of a ravine. The wind died down as the forest rose up on either side of them. Perhaps 'forest' wasn't the best term, at least not to Kasumi's way of thinking. What little plant life existed on Qaephar was no more than a dusting of tundra. The 'trees' of this forest were something else entirely; tall fingerlike sculptures of a gelatinous yet semi-hardened substance that resembled bluish-white amber. According to Velamar, a species of pervasive insect created the cylindrical formations in order to procreate. Judging from the forest's sheer expanse, they were one of the few creatures that thrived on Qaephar's harsh surface.

"There! Do you see it?" she shouted.

He could see it, too – the rising smoke in the distance where the ship had crashed. There was no telling how large the ship was, though from Velamar's estimate it had to be much larger than a simple scout or survey ship.

"We've a long way to go," Velamar shouted back sourly. She caught the subtext in his booming voice despite the wind. *We won't get back to the refuge before nightfall.* Hopefully Velamar had packed a tent, she thought. She tightened her grip around his waist as the crawler picked its way at a faster clip along the ravine.

It was nearly nightfall by the time they arrived at the crash site. A gigantic crater had obliterated an entire forest of the gelatinous trees. Pieces of wreckage were strewn about like scraps of forgotten silver wrapping paper from a cosmic giant. The ground here was level, and just beyond the crash site the forest way gave way to a patchwork of tundra. Some sizeable chunks of the ship seemed to have broken off and landed beyond the forest. This was where they started their search in the fading light. Activating the zoom on their goggles, Kasumi and Velamar looked for any sign of survivors. A thread of hope twined around Kasumi's heart for just a moment as they caught sight of a chunk of the ship more intact.

Rows of what appeared to be seats were exposed to the elements, the top of the compartment missing. Kasumi saw them. Rows and rows of seated bodies, their upper torsos sheared off. Hope died. A sense of loss took its place. How many? Thirty? Forty? No, there had to be at least 70 or more, and these were just the ones not vaporized in the crash. Whatever the ship had been, it was no small explorer vessel or merchant cargo craft. This has had been a sizeable transport ship.

After they had combed through the scattered wreckage for another hour, light was failing fast. Snow had begun to fall. Flaky clumps, some as big as Kasumi's fist, started to swirl down under the three-moon twilight. Meanwhile, the cold had turned from mildly inconvenient to a bone-numbing minus eight. It would hit minus thirty or lower before the night was through.

"We need to make camp," Velamar shouted. Kasumi pointed at a cliff-face with what looked like a shallow cave at its base. It would have to do.

Using the cave and cliff-face as a shield from the elements, Velamar erected the Arctic Environmental Unit (AEU). Once properly positioned, the tent-like structure expanded at the press of a button. Soon its insulated inflatable walls and roof extended above their heads. All things considered it looked almost cozy. Velamar pulled the flap aside. He pinned it in place as Kasumi helped him carry in the supplies. Their task complete, Velamar resealed it. Other than the incessant howling of the wind against the AEU, there wasn't much to hear. Kasumi unrolled their sleeping bags side by side on the crunchy-cold ground. Velamar slid an electric heat-pad beneath both sleeping bags. The welcoming heat sprang up like a volcanic aura.

"There, that's more like it."

She grinned. "And here I was going to rely on your body heat to keep me warm."

He gave her a suggestive look. "Who says you still can't?"

The innuendo-laced humor helped lighten the lead weight Kasumi still felt. She had seen pictures once, back on Earth, of the aftermath of a flight which had crashed near New San Diego. The thought of all those lives lost in an instant made her sick. Her training as an Earth Alliance fleet officer had prepared her to encounter death, true. That came with the territory of exploring the far reaches of space, after all. But somehow all the training in the world couldn't quite prepare a person for seeing death up-close and on such a scale for the very first time…

Velamar sat beside her. "A skaelelii vortex for your thoughts," he offered. She had been teaching him human idioms, and he had become fond of re-adapting them with concepts from his own language. Sometimes his verbal concoctions made her laugh. This one triggered only a faint smile. He put his arm around her.

"I know, not one of my best efforts," he admitted. He gave her a squeeze. She stared distantly, wondering who those people were. There hadn't been enough left of the ship so far to even hazard a guess at where it came from or which race had built it. There was one bright spot among the wreckage though.

"Kasumi?"

Kasumi's eyes refocused. She looked at him and tried to latch onto the silver lining in the midst of tragedy.

"Sorry, I was just thinking. Maybe tomorrow once we take a closer look we can find out where that ship came from." She paused, her mouth turning into a grim line. "If there are any survivors out there, what are the chances they survive the night?"

Velamar rubbed Kasumi's shoulder thoughtfully. "Not good, I'm afraid. There's not much we can do though. Visibility is next to nothing. The snowfall is ramping up. At this rate we'll be lucky to find much of anything by morning," he admitted.

Kasumi surged upright. "Then we can't waste time."

Velamar looked at her in puzzlement. "What do you mean?"

She took a step toward the outside. "I saw part of a communications array from that ship still semi-intact. It's not much, and I know it's a longshot given what you said about Qaephar's upper atmospheric density, but I might be able to fix it or re-engineer it to send out a message. I'm no chief engineer, but I can work my way around an array." He was frowning. That frown had only deepened.

She grabbed him by the arm to pull him up. "Come on, we're wasting time."

"It's too dangerous," he countered. "Besides, it would be decades before any human ever received it. You have to accept the fact that this is your home now. More than that though, as difficult as it is, you must also accept that your family and friends may never know what happened. I'm sorry." He stared at the ground. Something wasn't right.

"Vel, you know how much this means to me. Even if there's only one chance in a gazillion, I don't care. I still want to try. My entire family, my colleagues in the Galactic Fleet, they all think I'm dead."

Velamar leapt up, anger flashing in his eyes. "And if I let you go out there you really will be!"

Kasumi could tell from the panic in Velamar's eyes that this was more than just a simple case of overprotectiveness. "Vel, talk to me. Why are you overreacting?"

Looking like a prisoner about to march to his doom, Velamar patted the sleeping bag across from him. His gaze had turned somber. "Please, Kasumi, sit. There is something I must tell you."

The Earth Alliance officer eased herself down beside him. Pinpricks of anxiety and dread raced up her arms. Time was critical. The longer they waited to retrieve that array, the more likely it was to get buried and become impossible to find…

"When I told you about my people exiling me here, you feared me at first – and rightfully so. For all you knew I could have been some criminal. But when I told you that my people feared me because of my telepathy, that wasn't the entire story."

"It did seem extreme," Kasumi added, trying to hide her impatience. "With so few of you born that way, why they would fear you so much, put you each on such isolated planets all alone. So what didn't you tell me?"

He looked away and scratched at his right ear – a nervous tic that didn't go unnoticed.

"More than 50,000 years ago a powerful telepath emerged among my people. Ilzar the Cruel they called him. He ruled as an unstoppable tyrant for over 2,000 years before rebels finally overthrew him. This is the real reason that my people bear such suspicion for telepaths, and much antipathy too."

"Okay… but what does that have to do with preventing me from trying to contact my people?" she growled.

"My llorien brethren are not just fearful of telepaths. Most of them hate us. Although my people pride themselves on treating telepaths humanely, that doesn't change how they feel… or their well-justified paranoia. As a result, they ensure we stay isolated."

"Meaning?"

"They monitor the planets they place us on. They give us a lifetime of whatever supplies we need, allow us to live in luxury of a sort, but that is all. They covertly restrict every telepath's contact with the outside world. They will allow an alien ship to land on the planet of an exiled telepath, but they do not allow it to leave. If I attempt to send a message into deep-space, the lloriens will come down to punish me and probably kill you as part of that punishment." Velamar looked at Kasumi with a bitter sadness. "Qaephar may not look like it, Kasumi, but this is my gilded cage. Now it has become yours too."

The young Galactic Fleet officer didn't know what to say. She was speechless. Then came the fury.

"What else have you kept hidden from me? So all this time... when you said the *Dragonfly* was unsalvageable, buried in the depths of the lake with the rest of my crew, was that even true?"

Velamar nodded firmly. "Of course, Kasumi. I have *never* lied to you. Your ship did crash into Lake Zur just as I told you. By the time I reached it, you were the only one I could save. The pressure of the water had already flooded half of the compartments on your ship and life support systems were failing. It was all I could do to pierce the compartment where you were lying unconscious and then swim with you back to the surface."

Something still wasn't right. Kasumi could sense it. There was still something he wasn't telling her. Her mind caught a different thread and followed it.

"So your other four companions... the wives you've had... how did you even meet them? Were they all just unlucky survivors from other crash-landings on your planet too?" He must have heard the skepticism in her voice. She had stood up again. Her arms were folded across her chest as she stared down at him. He shook his head sadly, as if knew how she would react to what he would say next.

"No, Kasumi. The truth is that the Seekstone I have, it lets me enhance my telepathic powers. The four companions that shared their lives with me did it of their own free will. I communicated with them for a time until they came to know and care for me, and I for them. They knew what they were giving up."

"I don't understand." Kasumi's breath came out in little puffs, anger lacing her voice.

"Despite the remoteness of this planet, the Seekstone allows me to reach out into the depths of space. The powers-that-be who imprison me here do not know of it, and if they did I am sure they would take it from me. As much as I use it, though, I am seldom successful. Most minds are not compatible with mine, among your species included. But once in a while, I am not sure why, there is a sentient creature of another species I *can* connect with and understand using the power of the stone. Using my Seekstone, I knew, the moment your ship crashed, that you were inside… that your life was slipping away. I knew I had to find you and get you out before it was too late."

Kasumi's jaw was hanging open in disbelief. Her gaze toward him had morphed from skeptical to accusing.

"So not only did you lie to me about why I'm stuck on this godforsaken rock with you, you also could have reached out with your Seekstone to let other humans know I was alive this entire time???"

He stood up now, taking her by the shoulders and trying to soothe her. "No, Kasumi. It's not like that at all. Perhaps once in a decade, and sometimes not even in *several decades*, do I find a single mind that is compatible with my telepathy, someone whose mind I can read. You are one of a precious few, Kasumi. Even if I wanted to, I could not simply reach out and speak to a human on another vessel. For one, distance makes it impossible. I can enhance the range of my telepathic abilities with the Seekstone only so far. I am sorry,

Kasumi. I did not want to keep any of this from you, but I also did not know what good it would do, telling you all this."

The woman took two steps back, pulling angrily out of Velamar's grip.

"You've done nothing but lie to me this whole time. You want to keep me here, is that it? You never want me to leave."

Velamar just looked at her with a sinking bleakness. How could he tell her that seeing the betrayal in her eyes was cleaving his very soul?

~ * ~

Chapter 4
Desperate Act
~ * ~ * ~ * ~

Velamar did not know what to do. He could see that he was losing her. He could see the betrayal in her eyes threatening to turn to outright hatred. Could he blame her, though? To be doomed to live out one's life on a planet far from home, far away from loved ones, with only a strange alien as a companion? He should have known it would end like this. *I should have known* he thought bitterly.

And yet he would not give up. He loved this woman. He believed with every fiber of his alien being that he could make her happy, if she would but let him. Perhaps she could not have the life she had dreamed she would have, but she could have a life. A *good* life. So he did the one thing he promised himself he would never do again. He did the one thing that would risk everything. He lunged forward.

"Get away from me!" Kasumi turned and ran out into the gathering blizzard. But Velamar was fast. He caught her and dragged her back into the shelter. She struggled in his arms, kicking, elbowing and even punching, but he took the blows. He weathered the storm she threw at him until he saw his chance. Then he struck. He held her head in both hands and attempted to make the full connection, mind to mind. He transported his thoughts to her, made her see what he saw, made her feel what he felt. He opened himself to her, a level of vulnerability beyond any that any normal mortal creature could ever hope to understand.

Kasumi's eyes widened. She stiffened, then gasped, then passed out.

~ * ~

Sunlight from above. No, that was the reflection of the three moons filtering in through the canopy of the shelter.

It was early morning. The blizzard had gone. Kasumi didn't know, she just sensed it – sensed it in the quietude and the tranquility of sound, or lack of sound, enshrouding the AEU. Her eyes opened.

She felt body heat cocooning her. Behind her, she felt Velamar's three hearts beating out the soft rhythms of sleep. He had his arms around her. His scent, a comforting woodsy smell somehow combined with hints of coffee, lingered in her nose. They were in the same sleeping bag. The two of them barely fit. Like a tube of overfilled toothpaste, it stretched at the seams, its thermal patterns about to burst.

Kasumi lay there, completely still, deciding what to do. *Do I try to escape?* What was the point, though? There wasn't a useable ship to fly. More importantly though, and to Kasumi's profound shock, she realized she didn't even *want* to. She sifted through Velamar's desperate emotions, thoughts, and tormented regrets, all still freshly emblazoned in her mind. He had laid himself bare to her. Still overwhelmed but starting to process it all, Kasumi realized something.

She understood. She understood the choices he'd faced in a way that simple words just couldn't ever convey. Had he violated her mind? No, to Kasumi's relief, she didn't feel that way at all. He had just opened himself to her, the raw, unvarnished truths, whether noble or ugly. She knew that now and she marveled at what he'd been willing to risk.

He loves me she thought. *He loves me as much as he has loved anything in his 552 years of life.* It was crazy to think that, to be able to know that. Two humans could stay married for 50 years and die a happy couple and never truly know that on the level she now knew. Whatever telepathic link he had created with her, it had worked. Some things couldn't be faked. She trusted it. She trusted her instincts, her own mind and heart.

Kasumi turned over. Tears flooded her face. Those emotions were now overwhelming her even after she understood their meaning. Kasumi knew… Her parents, her brother, her colleagues in the Fleet… she would probably never see any of them again. But what she had left wasn't nothing. His love. A home of sorts. A planet with maybe undiscovered wonders, who was to say for sure?

"Kasumi?" Velamar's eyes opened. He had sensed her stirring.

~ * ~

He saw her face contorting with emotion. He saw forgiveness in her eyes but the most intense sorrow too.

"I'm never going to see my family again, am I?" she said. The last shred of her resistance crumbled. Her voice cracked. The look she gave him shone with the devastation of finally admitting the truth. From denial she'd reached a place of grief.

Originally, after her crash and after they'd grown close, she'd made peace with her predicament. She'd believed Velamar when he told her that the Anomaly which had ensnared her ship and spat it out near Qaephar was nearly impossible to chart safely. The chances that the Fleet would risk ship after ship and further disaster were admittedly remote, and Kasumi decided she could live with that. But there was still the possibility of rescue, at least in theory. There was still the possibility of contacting someone who might inform Earth that she was still alive. Even if Qaephar was light years and light years away from any of the trade routes, Kasumi clung to that hope. Now, to have that hope tantalize, thrown in front of her in the form of the damaged ship array in the wreckage – only to find out she was trapped not just by natural forces but by the purposeful will of an alien species – it was too much.

She sobbed uncontrollably and he just held her. He just held her until the very last spasms of pain wound their way shuddering through her slender frame. Eventually, her grief spent, she relaxed in his arms. Her wet face nuzzled his neck.

"I'm sorry I was so angry," she sniffed.

"You had every right to be angry with me. I kept the truth from you," he whispered.

"Yes, but you had your reasons."

"Reasons are no excuse," he continued.

"They are when the reasons are beautiful," she said simply. Sensing the odd way that sounded, she soldiered on. "I know how much you love me now. I finally understand." She looked up at him, the trails of half-dried tears glistening on her face like jewels.

"I promise you this, Kasumi. If we can find a way to safely contact your people, we will. If I can make a telepathic connection with someone to contact your people to tell them that you're OK, that you're safe, I will."

It was a one-in-a-billion chance. Ten, twenty years might pass. Unless they could find a starship captain willing to navigate the near-certain death of the Anomaly, that hope was just a pipe dream. They both knew it. But he sensed how much she loved him for saying it. For keeping that hope alive.

"I'm so tired, Vel. Don't make promises you can't keep, all right? Just do me one favor."

He stroked her jet-black hair and kissed her, tasting her sweetness and her tears.

"Anything," he murmured.

"Hold me." Her smile faltered but didn't die. "If I'm going to live in a cage, gilded or not, I'm glad it's with you."

~ * ~

Chapter 5
Not Quite Empty-Handed
~ * ~ * ~ * ~

It was late morning and the whiteout conditions had dispersed. Qaephar's plummeting temperatures had crept back up too. At a balmy 30 degrees Fahrenheit, Kasumi and Velamar ventured out to explore what was left of the crash site. Snow drifts ranging up to nine feet deep now obscured much of the scene. Based on the whims of the wind, though, some parts of the ship's wreckage remained surprisingly salvageable.

Velamar took a few of the smallest pieces from the wreckage and put them in his pack. When Kasumi gave him a curious look, he added. "When I get back home, I can use the Seekstone to enhance my telepathy and sense what happened. The residual psychic energy from any part of the ship, even the outer hull, should be enough."

She nodded. No wonder he had been so protective of that blue-veined ivory crystal and never let it leave his study. It was his only lifeline to the outside world, she knew that now, but apparently it enhanced his powers in more ways than one too. What other telepathic abilities could he activate or enhance while channeling it? She couldn't help but wonder.

Unfortunately, despite a thorough survey of the forest and surrounding tundra in daylight, they found no survivors. The two then approached the larger section of ship with the 70 or more headless occupants for a closer look. At the last moment, though, Velamar steered them aside.

"What's wrong?" Kasumi asked.

"Something's not right." He grimaced. "We shouldn't go any closer." When she gave him a searching look and begged for more explanation, he held firm.

"When we get back home, I can confirm what happened to the ship. I have the wreckage fragments. We don't need to inspect the bodies.

I'm picking up something residual from the psychic energy from the corpses. Something troubling…"

"As in…?" Why did he have to sound so damned mysterious?

"As in, I'm not sure, but something terrible happened to these people *before* the ship crashed." He paused, his grimace now even more entrenched. Kasumi knew what he was doing. He was seeing a series of disjointed and even fragmented images. Leftover memory-shards from the dead. Yet again she reminded herself that telepathy could be more curse than blessing.

"OK. Let's turn back," Kasumi agreed. There was a haunted look in Vel's eyes, as if he'd seen those frozen corpses strapped into the seats of the wreckage die all over again. For the first time, Kasumi truly realized the burden Velamar carried. Telepathy was often his only relief from loneliness, true, but it could be a lifeline to horror just as easily as to worthwhile connection or comfort. Kasumi felt a sudden determination to get Vel away from here – to take his mind elsewhere, to somewhere better. And that's when she had an idea.

They returned to the AEU. The sleeping bags and heat-pad were still unrolled and splayed out in the center of the enclosure. The wind had died down outside, now just a gentle whisper rather than a hiss or howl. Velamar began to busy himself getting ready to load up all of their supplies back on the crawler. Kasumi grabbed him by the elbow.

"What is it?" he murmured. She stared at him until the grimace he had been maintaining slowly softened.

"I'm sorry you had to see that… what happened to those people, or flashes of it anyway. Listen, I want you to know… about last night and earlier this morning…"

He looked away, clearly still uncomfortable about all that had passed between them.

"Please do not mention it. I was wrong to keep secrets from you. I thought I was protecting you when in reality I was just being selfish. I didn't want to have those hard conversations with you, and the longer I put them off, the more I rationalized it. I was in denial. I think I convinced myself that I could put off the inevitable forever."

Kasumi cupped the alien's face. "Vel, look at me. That doesn't matter now. I meant what I said before. I'm sorry I was so angry with you last night, and yes, I'm going to have some trouble adjusting to my new circumstances... but you know what? We'll get through this. OK?"

He nodded, but a haunted somberness lay across his brow as if he couldn't quite believe her, or worse yet – knew of some darker secret still lurking beyond her comprehension.

~ * ~

~ * ~

Chapter 6
Forgiveness
~ * ~ * ~ * ~

"Vel? Is there something else you need to tell me?" He had laid himself bare to her during the mind-share last night, but the onslaught of his emotions and their imagery had been too much for Kasumi to fully absorb. Even now, she found that much of the crystal-clarity from all his shared memories had started to fade. She still trusted him, but she felt she was losing a part of that intimacy. Perhaps she could convince him to share his mind with her and practice that same openness again. But she sensed too what a toll it had taken on him and she *knew* damned well that it had taken a toll on her.

"Kasumi, I… what I did was foolish and selfish, mind-sharing with you. My people, we call it the *shyam-shayek*. It's considered a sacred bond of intimacy between llorien lovers. It's—"

"SHH. No more apologies from you. That's an order." She paused. The idea from earlier resurfaced. She turned it over in her mind.

I can't think of a better way to get his mind off of all the death he's seen out here, and not just seen but felt *too.*

It was time to make Velamar feel something else, for him to know, with absolutely certainty, that Kasumi forgave him. Kasumi began to shrug out of her clothes, disrobing one layer at a time. Velamar gaped.

"Kasumi, what are you doing? It is cold in here. Perhaps not as cold as outside, but still, it's—"

"Then I guess you'll have to warm me," she murmured, arching an eyebrow.

Let me show you that I still love you, Vel. Let me do this for you.
Moments later, Kasumi was naked. She shivered, goosebumps erupting along both arms. He crossed to her. A sudden decisiveness

had taken hold of him. The alien pulled her to him, his mouth diving to hers. His lips captured hers in a bruising tenderness. His parka-clad figure wrapped around her. His hand strayed downward. Lightning raced along Kasumi's clit as he stroked her sex. She moaned into his mouth. Then he was stepping back and disrobing too. She shoved him a little. A playful glint sparkled in her eyes. He laid back on the sleeping bags. She came over to him, the aura of warmth from the electric heat-pad banishing what was left of the goosebumps.

She knelt between his legs. She took his thick cock between her slender fingers. It was already fully aroused. A whitish-clear fluid leaked from the tip in a constant trickle. It was like pre-cum for a male human, except the drip of fluid never stopped as long as he stayed aroused. It was designed to trigger arousal in a female of Velamar's species, but it seemed to work not just for lloriens… humans too.

Kasumi pumped the base of Velamar's cock with one hand. Soon her hand was soaking wet with his fluids. The sound of wetness as she pumped up and down, jerking his manhood, filled the chamber. She marveled at it. Its size. Its smooth yet masculine contours. The strong scent of him wafted to her nostrils. He had two heavy testicles. They were bigger than any human's. Her other hand gently massaged and stroked those wrinkled folds as she watched him get more excited. He lay there, staring up at her, letting her take control.

Now the slender human ventured to lean down yet further. She had never sucked his cock before. Kasumi flicked the tip of her tongue across his glans. A sweetness greeted her tastebuds. The fluids leaking from the tip of his shaft tasted almost like watermelon. She began to lick at his cock now, loving the taste of him. Then she took the next step. Kasumi's lips formed a firm seal around Velamar's cock-head as she began to suck. The explosion of flavor on her tongue was beyond anything she would have imagined. She kept going. Her mouth began to pump back and forth, taking in more and more of his cock. The naked woman could hear Velamar's labored breathing.

~ * ~

Velamar watched that beautiful face bobbing on his cock. He looked up at the woman tormenting him. His precious Kasumi. His companion. His beloved.

"Kasumi," he moaned. She was sucking now and more. She was pumping her mouth up and down at a furious pace, not just sucking but slurping too, drinking up his fluids as if they were a life-giving delicacy. Her hands were now both massaging his testicles, her jet-black ponytail bobbing up and down, up and down. Bliss wove about the telepath. The residual memories he'd sensed at the crash site dissipated and vanished from his mind altogether. He had only thoughts for this extraordinary woman. How could she be so versatile, so willing to forgive him after all he'd done? So confident that their relationship would not just survive but thrive despite his deception of omission?

Wet sounds of suction and arousal intensified. Kasumi's mouth was halfway down Velamar's shaft, but it would get no further. The llorien's cock was simply too tall and too thick. Kasumi settled for gurgling halfway down his length. Her gaze locked with his. There was so much love there it took Velamar's breath away. Those eyes of hers seemed to be saying *It's okay! I want you to come. Come for me.* Stubborn, though, Velamar held back. His forehead creased with effort. His hands clenched with determination. The churning seed in his alien testicles stayed where they were for now.

~ * ~

So he wants to play hard to get. Kasumi's tongue lolled downward, lapping at the underside of Velamar's cock. She came off of his cock with an audible pop as fluid oozed down her bottom lip.

"You taste amazing," she said huskily. Then, with an evil smirk, she proceeded to lean forward until his erect penis rested between the cleavage of her breasts. Smashing her breasts together against the sides of his manhood and lacing her fingers together, she began to move her torso up and down at a frenetic pace.

"Kasumi," he said with a tone of warning. A half-groan, half-unintelligible plea soon followed.

"Come for me, Vel. I want you to come. I love you so much. I want to feel the seed of the one I love on my skin. Please come, Vel. Come all over." Those words, with her breasts shaking as she bobbed up and down with his cock entrapped between her supple orbs, seemed to be his undoing. Velamar let out a plaintive wail. Kasumi gasped as the llorien's gigantic cock spurted violently. Huge ropes of cum splattered against her chin, but as she leaned back and opened her mouth the twitching member kept spewing. More ropes of cum shot across Kasumi's forehead, nose, and cheeks, but the lion's share of the prodigious load of alien seed landed on her perfectly sculpted breasts. Thirty seconds passed before Velamar's salvo was finally exhausted. By then, Kasumi glistened almost as if she had taken a swim in a vat of Velamar's jism.

His cum oozed down her face. She had to close her eyes and carefully wipe away the fluid just above her eyelashes. Staring down at the sticky mess she'd become, she could only marvel. Then, as seductively as she could, the woman began to gather up swaths of cum with her fingers and lick the fluids off of them as if she were sampling the rarest and finest dessert.

~ * ~

Velamar was mortified. More than that, though, he was *satisfied*. His cock lay wilted against his pelvis, happily spent, as he stared up at this incredible female. Such a capacity for selfless kindness and love she'd shown him. She had covered herself in his seed to prove a point, a point he finally and fully understood.

She forgives me. It was an extraordinary gesture. He had opened himself to her when he had shared his feelings and memories through the mind-share. Now she was returning the favor, showing a willingness to be intimate without shame, just showing how much she cared for him. Velamar sat up and pulled her to him. He kissed her, tasting the mingling flavors of her saliva and his own seed on her tongue. Then he laid her down beside him and slid two fingers against her pussy. Kasumi's eyes bulged at the onslaught of sensation. He covered her mouth with one hand even as he continued to finger her throbbing clitoris with the other.

"SSHH, my sweet little human. It is *my* turn to give *you* pleasure, so don't try to resist."

He loved the way she was panting against the palm of his hand. He kept it there, lightly over her mouth, gazing into her deep brown eyes. He watched her abdominal muscles twitch and shudder as his fingers did their sacred work. He stared lovingly into his human's eyes as she panted faster and faster. Her back began to arch instinctively as her legs widened further, her cunt bucking against his fingering invasion. He had two digits inside her now, pumping into her, while his thumb encircled her needy little clit. He almost had her now, he could sense it in the way she trembled and the way her heart pounded in her chest.

"PLLSSS!" Kasumi moaned, his hand still covering her mouth. *Please. Yes, Kasumi. That sound is the sweetest music I'll ever need to hear, even muffled against my hand. And the puff of your precious breaths of air against the palm of my hand is a sensation I'll never forget either. Each breath of air from your lungs is a treasure, sweet Kasumi, because I love you and all that you are.*

He had her now. Her nipples had pebbled up at the height of arousal. She was bucking violently into his finger-thrusts, grinding her clit against his thumb. She was breathing so hard now. He loved the sight of her chest heaving faster and faster. Her eyes rolled up in her head as she screamed into his hand, her cunt convulsing. Fluid gushed from her pussy and drenched his fingers as she clamped both of her hands down on the wrist of the hand stroking her. Soon the woman's overly sensitive pussy was begging for relief even as she came down from the orgasm. She looked up at him with grateful yet pleading eyes as he finally took his hands away from her mouth and sex.

"Oh my god… I've never come so hard before… you're a monster," she huffed, still breathing hard, looking up at him in wonderment. Somehow her midnight hair had spilled out of its ponytail.

He drew his hand away, now covered in her feminine fluids, and held it up as damning proof. "Who is the real monster?" he countered. "This addictive nectar is clearly the work of a powerful creature," he teased back at her, licking up her fluids and savoring the flavor and scent that was pure Kasumi.

"But as frightening a creature as you may be," he joked, "I think I am ready to tame you after all."

Kasumi looked down, her eyes widening a little at the sight of his reinvigorated manhood. As he settled his body atop hers, she opened her legs even wider for him. His cock lanced through her sated silken folds, driving deep until just his testicles showed. He froze. He relished that snug fit. Then he began loving her, his body swimming inside her, cock stroking her core to the hilt. And now Kasumi slid her graceful fingers along her lover's back. She looked into his eyes and the thought in her mind was so loud that Velamar read her thoughts even without trying.

Yes! Yes! Oh Vel, YES!!!!

~ * ~

Sometime later, the bulk of a naked llorien stirred on top of the naked human female pinned beneath him.

"You almost crushed me," she pouted as he eased off of her with a sigh. Propping his head up on one elbow, he looked down at Kasumi. Her naked body was laid out beside him like a priceless tapestry. A not inconsiderable amount of his seed now oozed down her sex all the way to the crack of her ass. Meanwhile the cum coating her supple breasts and neck had not yet dried.

"I think you're going to need a shower once we get back."

"Oh, shut up. Don't sound so proud of yourself. You made this mess. I should make you be the one to clean it up." Velamar leaned down, his hand cupping her sex, loving the feel of her heat throbbing against his palm.

"It would be my pleasure, woman, but I warn you that I may falter in my task, and then you would be back at square one."

Kasumi gasped as she felt the warmth of his hand against her pussy.

"Fair point," she said carefully. "Now get off me, you big ox, and go pack up the supplies."

"What is an ox?" He could tell her command lacked bite. The way she stayed so still, letting him continue to touch her, her jaw slack and eyes tender, told him all he needed to know.

"A very large, very dumb animal back on Earth," she whispered, her voice faltering as his fingers caressed her gooey cunt and clitoris.

He grinned. "Indeed, and you have the temperament of a yezrati matriarch in heat."

"I don't know what a yezrati matriarch is," she whispered back huskily, "but if you keep doing that, I'm going to need you to do me a favor."

"Name it. Anything," he murmured. She looked down at his cock, already re-energizing for a first-ever round three.

The Earth Alliance officer shoved his hand away. "Get on your back again." He complied, hands pillowed behind his head as she straddled him. Now she was grasping his hot penis between her delicate fingers, positioning it, sinking down on him. She let out an exhale of bliss as her sticky-slick warmth entrapped him. The wet sounds of suction and friction filled the AEU as she bounced on his cock. Clear-whitish fluid leaked from Velamar's manhood, coating Kasumi's pussy as she impaled herself, a waterfall of lust that soaked his lap. His pre-cum kept her so sticky that the sounds of wetness soon grew even more deafening. Each time she rose off of him his glistening-soaked shaft was visible for only a moment. Then she slammed back downward with a wordless coo and an echoing *splat*. Her nipples hardened, aching to be caressed or sucked. Instead, she just reached out, her hands splayed against his chest. She looked down at him as she fucked him, made love to him.

Their bodies joined. Their souls touched.

I don't deserve her he thought. *I risked her life and she doesn't even know it.* Perhaps he wasn't exactly a monster. It didn't matter though, because he was something far worse.

A coward.

~ * ~

Chapter 7
Riddle of the Passengers
~ * ~ * ~ * ~

"That's the last of it." Kasumi finished setting down the last supply-satchel from the snow-crawler. Velamar meanwhile had just finished his systems check on the crawler to ensure it would be good to go the next time they needed it.

Now hefting the pack with the pieces of wreckage, Velamar made a beeline to his study. He was all focus. He sat down. He dumped the pack's contents. Then he proceeded to place one hand on the Seekstone and one hand on the ship's remains. He closed his eyes.

Guessing that this might take some time, Kasumi tiptoed her way toward the shower.

The shower, compact as it was given the low ceiling, felt almost like a cave, but a cozy one at that. The painted stars on its gridstone walls shimmered in the half-light and reminded her of glow-worms she'd once seen on a trip to New Zealand. Staring at them had a calming effect. Kasumi's explosion of anger at Velamar and her attempt to flee now seemed to belong to another lifetime. Now she felt closer to him than ever. On the flipside, though, Kasumi felt a trace of disappointment that the last of the mind-share seemed to be wearing off. She could still remember her reactions to the memories, thoughts, and emotions he had managed to temporarily fuse into her brain, but as for the memories, thoughts, and emotions *themselves*? The parts of him shared to her psyche? All of it was fading. *Why do I feel like I just came off of a drug-induced high?*

But for Kasumi the attraction to Velamar was based on so much more than that. As a communications officer and linguist, the concept of language through visual telepathy intrigued her. *Perhaps that's why I fell in love with Vel so easily* she thought. He hadn't just shown himself to be a caring person strong of heart. He fascinated her too.

And yet... she had so many questions. Unresolved issues she desperately wanted to raise. How often did the lloriens send Vel supplies? Assuming it wasn't just once every decade or three, couldn't he at least get a message through? Couldn't he at least convince or bribe one of the pilots to find out if there might be a way to contact Earth? To let her family and the Earth Alliance know that she was alive? Then his words came back to her.

"I promise you this, Kasumi. If we can find a way to safely contact your people, we will."

It seemed an ironclad and solemn oath. But as Kasumi stripped out of her clothes and stepped into the sluicing heat of the pummeling water, she began to feel less sure. 'Safely' was the key word there. Would Vel tell her of a way to contact her people if it involved any risk to her whatsoever? She had a sinking feeling that answer could very well be 'No.' He was protective of her. That could be sweet at times. But there was a darker side to it. Not possessive... nothing like that, but still an 'I know best' streak that ranged from bothersome to infuriating.

The Earth Alliance officer closed her eyes and let the warmth of the shower embrace her like a lover. Thoughts swirled in her mind much like the water swirling down the drain.

I need to find out from Vel what's really possible. Didn't his four previous companions bring their own ships? Even if the lloriens were monitoring Qaephar, it was a big planet with a dense atmosphere. If one of Vel's previous companions had piloted a ship that could safely navigate the planet's atmosphere in order to land, it stood to reason that there would be a way to fly back out of orbit. The two of them could escape this gilded cage together, perhaps, if he would listen to reason. Of course, that assumed that Velamar's previous companions hadn't arranged to be cast down to the surface via one-way pods, or that their ships, now decades or possibly hundreds of years old, still even functioned.

And where would we even go? All that her plan would accomplish would be to make Velamar a fugitive. She would still be no closer to

Earth and no closer to contacting Earth Central Command or her family. It truly was hopeless. She let the spray of the water scatter her thoughts. There was something soothing about the heat. Sometimes it felt better not to think. Not to feel. Just to be. Just to forget.

"Kasumi?"

Steam billowed out past the glass door now sliding open. She hadn't heard Velamar step into the bathroom behind her.

~ * ~

"You're using up all the water," Velamar teased. Given the reservoir of water underneath the ice, that seemed hardly likely.

She didn't smile. Not even a faint imitation of one. He sensed her sorrow. It oozed from her like pus from a wound. Velamar had marveled at Kasumi's resilience earlier. Her optimistic insistence that they would 'get through this' back at the AEU had astonished him. Even without invading her mind, though, his telepathic senses and his instincts detected a resurging sadness. Not just sadness, but a profound disappointment perched on the edge of a much darker and deeper abyss. He turned her toward him.

"Is there anything I can do?" He hated this feeling of helplessness. The other companions he had lived with and loved – they had been here of their own choosing. They had fled lives that had grown oppressive, or just wanted to make a fresh start. They had yearned for a simpler, peaceful existence that he could provide. Not Kasumi. Kasumi had been forced. Forced by the hand of fate. *Maybe that's the difference* he thought. Maybe that was why no matter how much love he showed her, he still felt that it would never be enough.

"I wish there was," Kasumi murmured. "I know none of this is your fault, Vel."

"That doesn't make it any easier to see you in pain," he replied. He hugged her close. The steam and the spray hugged them in its own way too. He stroked her slickened hair. "Kasumi, I promise you it will get easier."

"I think that's what part of me is afraid of," Kasumi admitted. She began to cry again. She seemed to be crumbling all over again, letting the fresh wave of grief throw open the floodgates to her heart. At least now the spray of the shower could help wash away her tears. In that moment Velamar realized something though. Kasumi's recovery wouldn't be a single event. Her transition to this new and alien life wouldn't be a single snap of the fingers or a one-time breakthrough. Like most things in life, it would be a *process*. She would gradually learn to live with her new reality. It would be a journey of three steps forward, two steps back. Progress seldom wove in a straight line and grief stole back into the heart unexpectedly long after you thought you'd left it far behind.

"It *will* get easier."

"How can you possibly know that?" Her puffy eyes stared desperately into his.

"Because I know the profound depths of loneliness, Kasumi. Perhaps I can't fully understand what you're going through, but I know one thing. That pain in your eyes, I've felt that pain. I know what's like to be so alone that the world around you seems to be painted in shades of gray, brown, and black. Kasumi, please believe me. Will you be strong with me? Or, barring that, will you let me be strong for both of us for a little while?"

She kissed him. Kissing led to more. He picked her up. Her glistening legs hooked around his buttocks. Then he was inside her. Their bodies joined, he bounced her on his cock. Their mouths melded together. The shroud of steam and heat swirled around them as love and passion created a less tangible but no less potent warmth of its own. They didn't last long. Both were still exhausted from their journey to the crash site. Kasumi moaned. She shuddered, her body clamped to his, and he grunted, his manhood twitching in the throes of release. Their slickened bodies finally stilled together as one.

He let her down gently. She cleaned herself again, then took one of the nano-fiber towels off the hook on the wall. Velamar watched her dry herself off. Soon after, her naked figure vanished into the bedroom. He finished soaping and rinsing. Then, donning his softest night-robe, he strode into the bedroom after her. There she was, cuddled beneath the heavy comforter. When he walked over to check on her, though, Kasumi was already fast asleep. The tempest of emotions had taken its toll on his exhausted human.

He stroked her brow ever so softly. *May you find the solace you need.*

Returning to his study, Velamar decided to complete his unpleasant work. One hand on the Seekstone, the other on the crippled shards of ship debris, he sought the answer to the riddle – what had killed those passengers long before the crash? So far it had been slow going. He expected it would take many more hours to piece together the fragmentary imagery.

Not so.

Velamar cried out. The Ilorien bolted back out of his chair. In the process both he and the chair nearly tipped backward onto the floor. Kasumi came running. Velamar staggered, nearly fell, would have if she hadn't caught him.

"Vel, what's wrong?"

He turned, face lined, eyes etched in pain.

"I know what happened to them, Kasumi."

Her eyes widened.

Part of Velamar kept screaming inside because it was worse than anything he'd imagined.

~ * ~

Chapter 8
Enemy Unlooked For
~ * ~ * ~ * ~

Kasumi righted his chair and helped him ease back into it.

"Talk to me, Vel."

The alien's eyes returned to focus, but those two vivid, dark-gray orbs stayed haunted.

"What killed those people was a virus. Not just any virus," he growled, loathing in his voice. "A sentient virus. When I used my Seekstone, I could sense not just the thoughts of the dying but the virus's thoughts as well."

Kasumi didn't know what to say until panic bubbled up.

"Were we exposed?"

Velamar shook his head. "No. It spreads from airborne transmission at warmer temperatures." Velamar's face clouded over, gloomy as the dilapidated door to an ancient Skrelian tomb. "It attacks the lungs. It chokes its victims. It drowns them in their own fluids." The alarm and fear in his voice reminded her of their argument at the crash site.

The woman eased onto his lap and slid her arms around his neck.

"Vel, look at me."

There was something there behind his gaze. The deep of a darkness spliced with terror. Before she could prompt him further though, his next words were already tumbling out.

"Do you know what else I could sense, Kasumi? I felt it gloating. I felt its *euphoria*. I know where it is, too. I know the planet where it first thrived, where it first evolved. As we speak its raging through all the populations on a planet called Orghov VI, a planet torn apart by civil war. And soon every other planet in that system will be infected. Soon it will spread like cosmic radiation to stars near and distant.

Kasumi frowned. Her first thought, impractical as it was, returned to the ones she loved.

"We have to warn someone. We have to warn Earth."

The bitter laughter, more a wheeze than anything, shook Velamar's muscled bulk. "There is no one to tell, Kasumi. My own people hate and fear me. Nothing I tell them will be believed. Not until it's too late." He reached out, his hand stroking her cheek. "What would you have us do?"

"*Something*," she answered, sliding off his lap. Pacing back and forth with clenched fists, her mind raced. "There has to be something we can do."

Velamar's ears turned the incandescent crimson of a llorien's agitation. Then he bolted upright like a man receiving the eureka breakthrough for his first invention.

"Perhaps there is." Gathering up his Seekstone, he slipped the crystal into a protective Kevlar-like pouch. Then he strode toward the hangar. Kasumi kept up.

"Where are you going?" He stopped, paused, turned with a look that said 'I'm going to regret this, but to hell with it – with all of it.'

"Nowhere, Kasumi. Not without you. We need to go back to the crash site. I need your help."

As they entered the hangar together, Kasumi felt the urgency flowing in her veins. "OK, what's the plan?"

Kasumi watched as he pulled out a heavy metal chest from a storage panel set into the hangar's floor.

"The bio-suits are in here. Help me open this." As they suited up, he kept talking. "It looks like we'll be needing to look at one of those corpses after all. More than one. The more the better," he said with a feral grin.

That startled the Earth Alliance officer. There was something new in his tone, something that had replaced the gnawing anxiety and the fear.

"Care to share?" she countered, surprised at the lift of hope she felt, as if she were a kite caught in a sympathetic breeze and that breeze was Vel.

"The closer we get to the dead remains of the virus, the people it touched and even consumed, the more of its thoughts and memories I can analyze," the telepath added. "Magnifying my power with the Seekstone, I'll learn exactly what I need to know."

Kasumi's eyes lit up. "How to kill it?"

He nodded. "How to kill it. Beyond the inner glow of its mental euphoria and dominance, even with the weak connection I gleaned through the pieces of wreckage, I could sense an insecurity there. It hasn't evolved without obstacle. It's had setbacks – other organisms within its home habitat which it's never been able to conquer. Some even *it* fears. The seeds of sowing its destruction are there, in its past, lurking in its own thoughts. I just need to find them."

Velamar fingered the protective pouch inside his suit which cradled the Seekstone. His most precious and fragile treasure, it had never even left his study, much less the refuge. Until now.

Kasumi locked the second gauntlet of her bio-suit into place.

"What are we waiting for then?" she asked. "Let's go find ourselves some corpses."

~ * ~

Chapter 9
The Only Hope
~ * ~ * ~ * ~

The wind shrieked like a horde of attacking interstellar ghosts. Just in time, the snow-crawler lurched into the safety of the hangar and the portal doors cycled closed. A rumble gripped the mountainside. The floor beneath them shook.

"Avalanche," the llorien explained. "Routine hazard."

To Kasumi's way of thinking something which felt like an earthquake had erupted beneath your feet could be called anything *but* routine.

"Glad you didn't warn me about those on our first outing in the crawler," the human quipped.

He smiled. "I wish I had. Maybe then I could have gotten you to stay put," he teased. Their light banter was misleading, a purposeful distraction from what had to come next.

As they began to decouple their bio-suits, Kasumi couldn't stop herself. It blurted out with a will of its own. "Maybe you don't have to do this. Maybe we can find another way." She didn't sound convincing though, not even to herself.

Ever so gingerly, Velamar took the protective pouch from inside his bio-suit and drew out the Seekstone. Its dazzling brightness shimmered with tendrils of lapis lazuli. They had found the corpses. It had given them the answers they needed. Now the only question that remained was one of sacrifice.

"No, Kasumi. This is the only way." The llorien's massive legs pushed forward as he shrugged out of the remainder of his suit and then helped Kasumi do the same.

Kasumi hated that this was the only way, but it felt good to be doing something. Not just something, but something which might help the human race and, who knew, maybe even the greater part of the galaxy. Still, their raised spirits rested on a slender thread. There was no guarantee that the llorien supply pilot would even believe them.

That was where Kasumi came in.

~ * ~

The llorien supply ship received the automated request from a planet called Qaephar from Subject 126, given name Velamar Azarune. A telepath's own matter-resynthesizers could provide for all conceivable daily needs, but sometimes, like any complex and highly sophisticated technological device, re-synthesizers needed repairs or wore out altogether. Apparently this was one of those times.

Wing-Adjudicator Xeros of the Iccutarra Monitoring and Defense Grid (IMDG) adjusted his heading. The llorien's stubby nose crinkled with disgust as he saw the planet looming into view. An ice ball of a planet. Minimal flora and fauna. Appropriately remote for one of the dangerous telepaths among his people to live out their existence in harmless luxury and obscurity. He glanced at a picture of his family, Zweylea and their two children. Their son's mottled blue patches had finally faded to an adolescent carnelian while their daughter's mottled patches had vanished altogether. It would be her birthday tomorrow. He would miss it. Damn these entitled telepaths, every last one of them.

Things began to go wrong the moment he entered Qaephar's atmosphere. First the ship's FTL drive core alert began to flash. At first Xeros guessed a simple malfunction, but a cascade of other system failures threw him into a panic. Checking his trajectory, he chose the safest landing place he could. A routine supply mission had turned into a fight for survival.

~ * ~

Kasumi resembled a speck across the wintry expanse. She huddled, waiting for the llorien supply ship to make its emergency landing. Crouched, her parka hugging her body with her hood up to ward off the wind and chill, she'd never felt more alive. She could be forgiven for forgetting even the cold as the temperature dropped to only a few degrees above zero Fahrenheit. There it was now, the squat, crab-like vessel. It was huge, the size of a house. Its landing feet extended out like claws, tunneled into and gripped the ice like the talons of an interdimensional dragon. Kasumi leapt out of her hiding place. She approached the emergency hatch and banged against it for all she was worth.

This was the riskiest part of the plan. It required curiosity. It required that the pilot be curious enough to open that hatch in the first place. She waited. She was too slender and too short to be a llorien. She posed no obvious threat. The pilot had to know that. The wind tore at her. Her face, enshrouded in two layers of wraparound nano-fiber scarf and a pair of snow-goggles, still felt the wind's bone-numbing slashes. Then she saw something. Or thought she did. She thought she saw movement on the other side of the porthole near what looked to be the ship's bridge. The emergency hatch slowly cycled open. It unfurled like the receding petals of a flower. There stood the llorien pilot, his energy-rifle raised.

"Please, I need your help." She had to shout to be heard. Between the muffling from her scarves and the screeching of the wind, could the alien even hear her? She unwound the scarves and put her hands up high. "Please don't shoot."

"I am not authorized to remove anyone from this planet. This is a Class-A Quarantined Planet with a dangerous telepathic subject in residence. Step away."

"I'll do whatever you want. I'm not asking to leave. But there is something I need to give you. The fate of your people, or at the very least *millions* of your people's lives, and many other races, depend on it." The pilot could see her face now. She then raised her hands even higher to appear more non-threatening. She squinted through the specks of ice which Qaephar's relentless wind lashed at her like an invisible whip. "Please, I'm asking nothing of you. I'm only asking you to hear me out."

The pilot regarded her dubiously. In the end, though, he jerked with the butt of his rifle in a terse invitation. She didn't wait for him to change his mind. As soon as she cleared the airlock, the hatch reversed, the metallic petals sliding back into a seamless shielding. The blizzard battered against the hull like muffled protests from the planet itself.

She looked at the llorien. He was bigger than Velamar. Way bigger. Velamar stood at around 6'3 to Kasumi's 5'7, but this alien had to be almost a full foot taller. If she was a hill, he was a mountain. His mottled face had streaks of color down either side. That was new to Kasumi, too; Vel didn't have any such coloration. Maybe it was analogous to human ethnic groups, some darker skinned, some lighter skinned. She'd have to ask Vel about it if she got through this in one piece.

"Speak quickly. I have a ship to repair and a schedule to keep."

"Your ship is fine," Kasumi said carefully. "Velamar tricked you."

The pilot frowned. "Impossible. My ship is shielded with–"

"He's a very powerful telepath. More powerful than any other telepath ever born," she rushed on. "He made you see what he wanted you to see." Velamar's Seekstone enhanced his telepathic abilities enough to penetrate the llorien ship's shielding, but she left that part out.

The llorien's hands tightened around his energy-rifle.

"Let's say I believe you. Why are you telling me this?"

"Because I am being honest with you. We had to get you down here on false pretenses, and for that I apologize. But there are lives at stake. Millions and millions, maybe billions."

"What are you to Subject 126?"

"His *name* is Velamar. My ship crashed here and he risked himself to save me. I know this is hard to believe because everything you've been taught tells you that telepaths are dangerous or even vicious, but he's no different from you or me. He saved my life. He's a good person. Now please listen. A week ago, a ship crashed here. It must have come through the Anomaly. It came from a distant planet called Orghov VI. The people onboard all perished in the crash, but in looking through the wreckage Velamar and I discovered that they were infected with a virus. Not just any virus…". She told him the rest, the gory details, as efficiently as she could. He listened with growing impatience at first, but then more intently.

This is it. The final sales pitch.

"This virus will spread everywhere and kill millions unless we do something to stop it." She pointed at the pouch belted to her waist. "Inside here I have a data-nub with everything we know about the virus, its weaknesses, and most importantly, a cure." She moved with exaggerated slowness, unhooking her pouch and sliding it to the pilot with her foot. The llorien leaned down and took it, but his eyes never left her.

"And why should I believe a word you say?"

"What do I have to gain?" she countered. "I'm going to stay here. I know the laws of your people. Those who violate the quarantine of your telepaths are doomed to stay with them. I accept my fate. But do you want to accept being the one responsible for killing millions of your own people? Do you have a family? Because if you do, that virus is coming, I promise you, and it will wipe out or decimate entire cities. Velamar has already seen it. He's experienced the virus' innermost thoughts, its triumphs, its cunning. What's your name?" she added.

The pilot regarded her quietly. The silence stretched for so long Kasumi almost thought he wouldn't answer.

"Xeros."

"Xeros, my name is Kasumi. I come from a place called Earth. I'm dozens of light years from home, a home I'll never see again. But I've learned to accept my life here and even cherish aspects of it. Do you know why? Because Velamar is worthy of my affection and yes, he's even earned my love. He's worthy of your trust too. All I ask is that you just ask yourself this simple question; if you have children, if those children die from a virus you *know* you could have helped *stop*, could you live with yourself? Could you?"

The pilot unlocked the pouch and fingered the data-nub within. He looked down at it, considering. He looked back at her. She sensed his struggle. The conflict between the ideology he'd been taught and what his instincts were telling him now.

"What is this cure you speak of?"

Kasumi nodded. "It's all in the data-nub. It's on a planet called Kyrax in the Bolian system just over a parsec from your homeworld. You know of it?"

Xeros nodded. "I do."

"On that world there is a type of fungus which is immune to the virus. More than that, this fungus *feeds* on the virus, consumes it as a source of energy. Your scientists will be able to use it to synthesize a cure."

The llorien pilot tucked the data-nub into his front vest pocket and threw Kasumi back her pouch.

"If I report Subject 126's actions today interfering with the operations of a llorien defense grid starship, do you know what will happen to him? My superiors may order him to be detained for experimental observation and you along with him. Or they may simply mark this godforsaken planet as off-limits and cease all supply support. You and this Velamar of yours will then be truly alone." The alien paused, scratching his ear thoughtfully in a way that reminded Kasumi of a man rubbing his chin.

"Or," Xeros continued, giving Kasumi a pointed look, "I might not have seen anyone here. I might have just landed briefly to repair a malfunction with my thrusters before dropping off the supplies and leaving orbit. On the way back I *might* happen to meet an unknown science vessel whose chief medical officer gives me this important data-nub with a warning to pass it on to my superiors." He let that hypothetical sink in. "That might happen too."

"That might happen too," Kasumi echoed. She didn't know why she did it; in retrospect it was foolish, really. Reckless. But she found herself walking toward him. He raised the energy-rifle. With her hands still up and palms open in a gesture of surrender, she came to a stop right before him. He lowered the weapon. The young Galactic Fleet officer looked him in the eye.

"Thank you." She wanted him to see her face up-close. To truly look at her. She could sense it, somehow. She knew. If trust sometimes balanced on the head of a pin, then so be it. Sometimes you had to take that risk.

"There are many lives in your hands, Xeros. Velamar's and mine are just two of many. Regardless of what happens to me and Vel, it will all be worth it if you do the right thing and make sure that the right people take a look at that data-nub. That's all I ask. That's all I care about. Other than that, do what you have to do. I understand."

He grunted. Kasumi wasn't sure if it was a good grunt or a bad grunt – a *'She's got nerve but I like her'* grunt or a *'The sooner I get this crazy alien female off my ship, the better'* grunt. Abruptly he cupped her chin, brought his forehead to hers and seemed to be trying to peer into her very soul.

"If you are lying to me, Kasumi of Earth, if this is a ploy to help your telepath friend escape his rightful place here, you will pay dearly for it. If so, you will share his fate, I promise you that. Do you understand?"

"Yes."

Uncomfortable closeness combined with uncomfortable silence. He seemed to be gauging the authenticity of that single word and the traces of truth or deceit behind her chestnut brown eyes. Then he nodded. "Very good then. Goodbye, Kasumi of Earth."

The llorien pilot pressed a button and the emergency hatch cycled back open. Flurries of snow and sleet created a whorl of motion that reminded Kasumi of the jaws of a beast ready to swallow her up. She turned to go. She put one foot in front of the other and just when her toes crossed the threshold between ship and snowclad footprint, he called out to her.

"Kasumi of Earth."

She turned. He wasn't smiling at her, not exactly, but he was looking at her with a bemused sort of grudging admiration.

"Take care of yourself and stay out of trouble. Oh, and most importantly – tell your telepath not to waylay any more defense grid starships if he values his skin."

She smiled, surprised at the gruff mercy of a soldier-pilot-stranger.

"You too," she called back. "Stay out of trouble. Next time take better care of those thrusters."

As she watched the llorien supply ship retract its claws and ascend through whiteout gusts, she said a silent prayer and sent it to join Xeros on his journey. What would happen would happen, but Kasumi felt oddly at peace. She and Vel had done what they could for now.

~ * ~

Chapter 10
Confession

~ * ~ * ~ * ~

Velamar picked up Kasumi in the crawler as soon as she activated the beacon by pre-arranged signal.

The whiteout lashings of Qaephar's latest blizzard tore at the crawler like a vengeful yezrati matriarch snubbed by a male during mating season. Luckily Velamar was used to working in poor visibility. Meanwhile the crawler's sensors helped him adjust.

"Did it work?" he shouted. His booming voice cut through the howling.

He couldn't see the potential smile underneath all those layers of scarf or the woman's goggles, but he did see the thumbs-up Kasumi gave him. Now he could finally banish the weight which had made his three hearts feel like tectonic plates grinding together. He took a breath. A deep, grateful breath.

It worked. It actually worked. I should never have doubted her. The disastrous what-if scenarios eclipsing Velamar's every thought had included the llorien pilot detaining her and taking her with him… or worse. With her hands cinched around Velamar's middle from behind, he felt enormous relief not only because she'd returned safely, but because they had accomplished what they had set out to do. A dangerous interstellar virus would at least not run unchecked through Orghovi space and the systems beyond – not if they and one open-minded llorien pilot had something to say about it.

They'd walked a tightrope of mistrust to do the near-impossible. They'd tipped the scales. Not bad for a day's work. *Not bad for a reclusive hermit-telepath-in-exile and a human castaway* he thought to himself.

~ * ~

"Kasumi, there is something I need to tell you."

Kasumi had just eaten the last savory bite of the sausage, spinach, and onion pizza he had made them for dinner. It was a perfect recreation from The Walloping Tomato, a pizza joint two blocks west of New San Francisco's Koreatown. With all of her memories vividly integrated into the telepath's own psyche, her childhood to adulthood spread out before him like a map, Velamar had made a decision. He'd decided to use his matter-resynthesizer to create for her all of the comforting foods she'd known from home and from her youth. True, she might not ever *see* her homeworld again. That did not mean that she could not experience it again. Through smell. Through taste. Through the other senses.

This meal is my last gift to you before you come to hate me, Kasumi. He would have to cherish this last happy moment between them and accept the bitter years to come.

The Earth Alliance officer rose from the table, the patterns along its dark wood grain surface gleaming under the glow-globe chandelier.

"Uh-oh. I'm not sure I like your tone. We have reason to celebrate. Are you sure you want to spoil it with a confession?" she teased. She sauntered around the table to him. Her hand stroked the nape of his neck. She had mischief in her eyes.

"Kas, I'm serious."

"So am I," she said. "You've earned a reward for helping possibly save millions of lives. We both have, yes?"

"No," he added darkly. "*You* have. *I* haven't."

She sat down in the chair beside him. She took one of his hands in both of hers. "OK. I'm here. I'm listening."

He heaved a dread-filled sigh. "The mind-share I did with you the other day at the crash site... it was dangerous. It was a desperate act done in the heat of the moment, and I was wrong to put you in danger. I was wrong to risk your life for my own selfish desires."

"I don't understand."

"As I was trying to tell you before, the mind-share, the *shyam-shayek*, is a special, intimate form of telepathic connection. Normally only another llorien mind is compatible for it. Originally I didn't know this." His gaze turned inward, haunted, shame-crippled. He couldn't get the next words out. *I haven't had just four companions, Kasumi. I've had five. My first companion isn't buried out on the terrace, and do you know why? Because she died after I initiated the shyam-shayek. Her mind couldn't take it. She went insane. She killed herself.*

She had a right to know the danger he had put her in, but the awful confession lodged in his throat now like the hemolymph from a Qaephari snow beetle. Cowardice gripped him. Finally, he said it. He spoke every torturous word wishing it were his last. She would never forgive him. He knew that. He knew her mind so well that he knew there would be only one possible outcome to the recklessness, selfishness, and cowardice he now revealed.

After the confession, nothing. Silence. Other than the howling wind, he could hear his own hearts beating. Kasumi had withdrawn her hands from his. She had stood up and taken several steps back.

She looked at him for a long time, her expression unreadable.

"If you could go back to the night at the crash site and do it all over again, what would you have done differently?"

He paused. She was searching for something in his answer, but what? "I would not have tried the mind-share with you. I would have pulled you back into the AEU with me rather than let you run out into the blizzard. I would have tied you down if I had to, to keep you alive until your fury cooled, and then? Then I would have taken you back to the crawler and brought you home."

"And then?" Kasumi prompted.

He still hadn't figured out what she was looking for. What did she want from his answer?

"Then... then nothing. Then I would have tried to earn your trust back, one painful day at a time while you had every reason to hate me and question my motives. Instead of doing the hard work of earning your trust back though, I took the shortcut." He looked away, clenched a fist and dug his own fingernails into his palm so viciously that blood trickled out. "I took the shortcut and you could very well have died because of it." He stared at her then, his self-loathing eclipsing his misery. "Now you see me for what I am. A coward."

Kasumi Ogawa gazed back at him for what seemed to Velamar the same amount of time it took all three of Qaephar's moons to complete their orbit – far too long.

Then the woman strode up to him. "Do you know what I see before me?" she murmured. "A person who's made terrible mistakes." She took his hand between her slender fingers and pulled it off his lap. "But you know what? I see someone else too. I see a person who was willing to risk his comfortable, solitary existence on a far-fetched ploy. I see someone who may have just helped save many planets' worth of lives from a vicious virus." She looked at him with an empathy that warmed him like a geothermal blast. "I see someone who did the right thing when the easy thing, the comfortable thing, the *safe* thing, would have been to just look the other way." She now reached out to caress the side of his mottled cheek. "You could have lied to me, Vel. You could have told me that you would send a message to your people. You could have chosen other paths to shield me from any possible danger. From possibly losing me. You didn't."

Kasumi brought the hand she held to her lips. She kissed his calloused knuckle with a tenderness that made at least two of his three hearts skip a beat. "When a crisis struck, you didn't hesitate to sacrifice what you wanted or what you valued most for yourself. That's not just the mark of a good leader. It's the mark of courage." She stroked the knuckle she had just kissed with feather-light fingertips. "Maybe you are a coward, Velamar Azarune. But if so, you are *my* coward. You are my kind of coward. A person who can admit his mistakes, wants to learn from them, and shows a willingness to sacrifice himself for others even when instinct takes over." She smiled then. "And you know what? I think in your own way when you did the mind-share with me you were actually trying to *protect* me. I think a part of you saw me in so much pain and just wanted to make it stop as quickly as possible. I think you felt not just my sense of being betrayed but also how devastated I was by it, and I think your instinct was to make me *understand* so that I wouldn't have to dwell in all that anguish."

Velamar exhaled with a relief he'd never known. He had thought he could read this woman after all he knew about her. Instead this marvelous, unpredictable human had just proved him wrong. Yet that didn't change the fact that he didn't deserve her – or her forgiveness. He tried to say as much.

"Kasumi, you put a positive spin on everything I've done, one which I cannot take credit for. The bottom line is that I risked your life. How is that any different from the high school boyfriend who wanted to take you drag racing with him despite the danger, not prioritizing your welfare? On some level I wanted you selfishly for myself. For a split second, I forgot about *your* welfare and fixated purely on my own perceived needs. There's no excusing that. There's no—"

Her finger pressed itself to his lips. Velamar's diatribe died on the point of that finger as if it were a spear.

"Yes, for a split second you did forget about my welfare. Part of you did. Do you know what I call that? I call that being *human*. And whether you like it or not, you big, dumb ox, I *choose* to forgive you. You don't get to decide how I feel or how I react to your idiocy. And if you don't like it, well guess what? That's too damned bad." She peered at him steadily, her eyes showing a compassion he still didn't think he deserved.

Finally he accepted it though. He accepted that he had no control, that as long as he was living with this extraordinary human, he would learn from her every bit as much as she might learn from him.

"I have been called many things," he rumbled, "but never *human*."

Kasumi pulled him up from the chair. Turning, tugging on his hand, she yanked him toward the bedroom and looked over her shoulder.

"Consider it a compliment," she said, her eyes bright. "Now come. Just because I forgive you doesn't mean I'm letting you off easy."

His brow wrinkled in confusion as she pulled him into the bedroom and manhandled – well, more like *womanhandled* – him onto the bed. He found himself being shoved onto his back. How did a twig-like human possess such strength? It defied the laws of physics.

She slipped off her shirt, bra-less underneath, erasing the thought. Erasing all thoughts, really. All except for one.

I am the luckiest fool who ever lived.

~ * ~

Chapter 11
Loving
~ * ~ * ~ * ~

"Don't move," the communications and linguist officer ordered.

Velamar lay there mesmerized as Kasumi undressed not just herself but him too. At last, both in their birthday suits, Kasumi began the most devilish and extraordinary campaign of teasing and tantalizing in the known universe. She leaned between his legs, her tongue flicking gently along the base of his cock. It stiffened, as vertical as the gelatinous trees scattered across much of Qaephar's surface. She did little more than that though. Occasionally her tongue would flick to his glans, teasing the tip. It had begun to leak its inexhaustible supply of pre-cum. The sweet scent of it filled the bedroom. Still she toyed with him using teasing flicks interspersed with licking and sucking on his heavy testicles while she languidly pumped the base of his shaft with one hand. This went on for nearly a half hour. Meanwhile the sounds of her slurping and sucking filled the bedroom like a kind of music. Kasumi finally started sucking on the tip of his penis, but only gently – edging him mercilessly as she stared at him with loving eyes.

Finally Velamar decided that enough was enough.

You've awoken the beast, woman. Prepare to reap the consequences. With a feral grin the llorien exploded into motion. Kasumi gasped as he got the upper hand. He dove behind her, then tossed her face down onto the bed. Before she could register what was happening, he tied both of her wrists to the headboard with her own discarded clothing.

"What do you think you're doing?"

But he didn't respond. He showed her instead. Kneeling behind her, the llorien began to lap at the young woman's bare sex. Kasumi stiffened. Her breath hitched. Then she began to breathe faster and faster as Velamar sucked at the folds of her pussy and ate her out feverishly from behind. Kasumi's head hung low as her cunt cream began to trickle onto the alien's eager tongue.

Yes, Kasumi. Surrender. Let me give you the pleasure you deserve. I don't deserve you. I never will. But you deserve this. You deserve all the bliss in the world – all that I can give you.

After a while, he withdrew. He loosened the knots, flipped her over, and retied her wrists. His stiff cock saluted her glorious body all the while. Then he dragged her further down the bed until her arms were taut. He spread her legs and dove between them. Velamar's mouth worked with a fervent intensity which knew no boundaries. He sucked on her clit. His tongue explored her silken tightness. He gripped her hips and feasted on her like an immortal elixir that could only be drunk once in a thousand years.

Meanwhile, Kasumi's breathing had grown ragged. His little human's nipples had morphed into tiny brown studs of need. She had begun to press her pelvis forward. The Earth Alliance officer nudged her cunt against his feasting mouth and lips.

"Ooohhhhh… Vel… Oh god…" Kasumi's next moan swallowed up the words. She began to buck against his mouth more firmly. Her entire body thrust itself toward him in needy ecstasy. He obliged. Velamar's teeth nipped at her clitoris. Then he captured it between his tongue and teeth, gave it a firm yet tender squeeze.

Kasumi's eyes rolled back. She arched off the bed. Her pussy convulsed wildly, spewing its fragrant fluids. Before she had even recovered, though, he pushed her up further on the bed and tied her ankles to the bed posts on either side.

"Uhhhh… what are you doing?" she asked through the haze of residual pleasure. He didn't answer. Once again, he decided to make his actions speak louder than his words. He began to slide his tongue along her slit. He stroked her nerve bundle and inserted two fingers into her wet pussy, thrusting into her at a steady pace. His cunt-licking and finger-fucking continued unabated until she was writhing in her bonds. A second convulsion shook her cunt. A second surge of her flavorful fluids rushed into his mouth. He lapped at her until his nose shone with her juices. Her taste, her scent – he reveled in it.

But still he wouldn't let up.

For the next hour he tormented her – the most exquisite torments imaginable. He feasted on her sex to a total of 12 orgasms. Each one seemed to him unique. The way her naked body shivered at his touch. The way Kasumi's eyes rolled back. The way the moan escaped her lips as she shuddered and came in his mouth each and every time. It was beautiful. It was glorious. It seemed a kind of perfection he had never known before.

Panting, gasping for air, after the twelfth orgasm Kasumi looked up at him with a silent plea. Then not so silent.

"Please Vel, I can't take much more."

Velamar stood up and walked beside the bed. His hand cupped her sated pussy. He loved the warmth of her beneath his palm – her stickiness too.

"Is that so? After all the teasing you did to me, I think you deserved this, don't you?"

"Consider me thoroughly punished then," Kasumi said, licking her lips. She stared at his cock.

He caught the hint.

"Oh, you want more?"

She nodded. A glint of mischief lit up her deep brown eyes. He felt an ache now as he took in her beauty, as he felt how much he loved her.

"You'll get more," he growled then. With an inferno of need and passion to spare, the muscular llorien undid her bindings. But not for long. Soon he had her on her hands and knees again, her wrists once more tied to the headboard. His calloused hands slid along her flanks. Then they glided up to the smooth skin of her lower back. They caressed the perfect contours of her ass cheeks. He positioned the bulbous crown of his cock at her wet, warm pussy. Kasumi looked over her shoulder at him. The need in her eyes screamed at him.

So of course he teased her. He stopped with just the tip of his cock inside her. Only the barest tip. Held still. Waited. She tried to throw her hips back and impale herself on his rigid member. He retreated, foiling her nefarious plan.

"Tsk, tsk. You are being naughty. Behave yourself, human."

Kasumi wiggled her hips and ass, grinding her pussy backward in every enticing way possible.

"Please!"

"Please what?" he asked innocently. His hand had settled along her pussy, gently rubbing her clit.

"Please fuck me!" Kasumi all but moaned. Now he had her. He knew how much she loved this, the buildup, the anticipation, even though she might claim otherwise. It was part of their now timeless dance. As their intimacy had grown so too had their camaraderie. Two lovers were lovers, but every bit as importantly, they were also *friends*.

"You mean make love to you?"

"Yes," Kasumi begged. "Vel, this is *torture. Please.*"

Velamar Azarune leaned over and undid his companion's ponytail. The jet-black hair which so fascinated him now spilled to her shoulders. He bunched it up in his fist, tugging on it– not too harshly, but just enough. Then he pulled her head back and inserted his cock at the same time. Pulling gently on her hair, he began to fuck her, using her body as leverage, slamming his cock deep into her softness. Kasumi's nipples hardened. She moaned and fucked him back. Her hips rammed backward to eagerly greet each and every pulverizing fuck he gave her.

"Ooohhh Vel, yes. Fuck my brains out. Yes. Fuck me. Oh god, fuck me, fuck me so hard, Vel. Aaaahhhhh!"

His little human was enjoying herself. Well and good. So was he. Now, thrusting his cock into the exquisite feminine sheath of Kasumi's sex, he felt whole. He felt the grace she had given him. She had forgiven him. She had allowed their intimacy to overcome all fears and the misunderstandings that could so easily develop between people of two different species. He was grateful to her. Velamar realized in that moment that he would never, ever be able to properly show her just how grateful.

But he would give it all he had. He would try.

Slamming into his beloved from behind, his testicles slapping against Kasumi's thighs, he felt her go over the edge. Kasumi's pussy tightened around his girth, squeezing desperately as the throes of ecstasy surged through her pleasure-fogged brain. He fucked her more violently now. His body slammed into hers at breakneck speed, the bed shaking beneath them as he reached for the pinnacle. Velamar's hand, still fisted in that lustrous shiny-black hair, yanked harder. Kasumi arched her back, moaning.

Then it hit him. Pleasure which could no longer be ignored or denied. His cock hurled forward like a battering ram and he stilled inside her, exploded in her with a fountain of warmth. His cum filled her, saturated the intimate depths of her cunt in a blast of viscous joy. He held himself there in Kasumi's pussy, waiting for the last spurts of jism to fling themselves toward her womb. At long last, the millions of llorien sperm in his testicles were spent. He pulled out with a sigh of bliss. Velamar then watched as the waterfall of jism oozed out of his beloved's pussy to pool on the bed.

Looking down, he thought to himself *even the mess we made looks beautiful to me.* It sounded crazy, but that didn't make it any less true.

He gave Kasumi's ass an affectionate smack. Next, surprising both of them given their mutual fatigue, once he had untied the ropes around her wrists, he signaled that he wasn't done. Not yet. Instead, he lay her on the bed face-up. He settled on top of her. His semi-flaccid cock lanced her cum-soaked silken folds. He felt his cock fitting into the snugness of her sticky sex with a surge of satisfaction.

Kasumi, I just want to stay here inside you forever.

There, atop her, he began to kiss her and Kasumi kissed him back passion for passion. Her hands stroked the back of his neck and the backs of his shoulders as he swam deep within her, his cock stroking her core. He kissed her forehead and then breathed in her scent as his cock slammed home once more into her welcoming sheath. They lay like that for a good hour, gently kissing and fucking, loving each other with infinite patience. From the frenzied lovemaking of earlier they settled into a tranquil joining of two bodies and two souls become one.

~ * ~

Chapter 12
The Seekstone
~ * ~ * ~ * ~

Kasumi woke up in bed and rolled over only to find nothing beside her except an imprint of Velamar's vanished form.

It had been nearly five weeks since their colossal gamble waylaying Xeros, the llorien pilot. For almost five frustrating weeks they had been playing the game of 'Wait and see.' Cut off from the outside world, they could only hope that what they had done would be enough.

Maddening doesn't even begin to describe it she thought ruefully. Slipping out of bed, the naked woman made her way toward Velamar's study. These days she was less and less self-conscious in Velamar's presence. Pretenses mattered little to her now. This refuge, this 'Turtle's Shell' as she liked to call it, Velamar's home encasing the mountainside much like a shell, had finally begun to feel like exactly that to her. Home.

Not that it erased the pangs of sadness and regret which stole upon her now and then. But the pain had become manageable. She had learned to thrive in her new place in the universe – even if perhaps it was far different than the one she had envisioned for herself a seeming lifetime ago… Far different than the one she had envisioned back in Galactic Fleet basic training when she had first put on that shiny new uniform.

"Here you are," Kasumi murmured. She stepped into the cozy and cave-like study. The candles burned low, aided only by the starlight from the tiny skylight above. Velamar was bent over the desk of his study. He was oblivious to her. His focus lay elsewhere, on the Seekstone, as it so often did. Only now there was not just one Seekstone but *two*.

"Is it working?" she asked.

He flinched, startled.

"What? Oh!" His eyes zeroed in on her naked breasts. His male gaze lingered on her curves before dipping to her bare pussy. Placing her hands on her hips, Kasumi stared with expectation.

"Are you just going to sit there ogling me or are you going to answer my question?"

Velamar seemed to recover his wits, if barely.

"Yes, it's made quite a difference, Kas. I think that with this second Seekstone I will be able to find another mind compatible elsewhere in the universe much more quickly. Already I am reaching out to new depths, to systems further than I have ever been able to probe with my mind ever before. Soon we will have some answers. Soon we will know what is happening outside of our own little bubble."

She smiled at him. Then her gaze drifted to the damaged communications array which sat on a workbench at the opposite end of the study. That had become her workspace now. Her own little project. She had been tinkering with it for several weeks now, ever since Velamar had insisted on going back to the crash site and retrieving it for her. He made her promise not to try to send out any messages and she'd agreed. Just to be able to tinker with it though gave her something to occupy her mind. Velamar's endless library of translations and alien languages gave her plenty else to enliven and occupy her time too though. She had entire worlds to explore entrapped within everything from the pages of ancient tomes to the pixels of terabytes upon terabytes of digital narratives on Vel's data-nubs. Stories. Knowledge. She had lifetimes of both at her fingertips. Life was cozy here, perhaps, but never dull.

And when the occasional stirring of cabin fever stole through one or both of them, the solution was simple. They geared up and prepped the snow-crawler. The occasional frostbite-prone adventure on Qaephar's surface provided a much-needed outlet when nothing else but a physical challenge would do. Of course, that wasn't the *only* physical extracurricular activity that they had learned to enjoy together.

"I'm glad to hear it," Kasumi added. "When do you want to go on another expedition?" Velamar's prediction remained fresh in her head – that a third Seekstone would increase his telepathic powers exponentially.

He grimaced. "I'm still recovering from our last outing. Nearly getting ourselves killed isn't something I can easily forget," he reminded her.

OK, so the cave ceiling had fallen in on them, and yes, she had had to help pull Vel to safety. But they would be more careful next time. She reminded him of that.

"Humph. So you say." He added an extra grunt for good measure. The grunt was noncommittal and filled with skepticism.

Kasumi realized something then. For the first time since crash landing on Qaephar, she was actually *happy*. Or perhaps *content* was a better word for it. As Vel had let himself open up to her, she had felt more and more like this was her place – being at his side, being here on Qaephar. That was why this place felt like home to her. And it wasn't just that; the Seekstones gave her renewed hope.

The Seekstone was another mystery Velamar had finally revealed to her more fully. Another one of Vel's secrets finally shared. He had revealed that the Seekstone came from a crystal formation he had found on Qaephar itself after first being exiled here. It was a geological phenomenon unique to this planet as far as he knew. From there she had interrogated him with growing curiosity and convinced him that where there was one crystal there might be more. Despite the dangers in spelunking through icy caverns underneath Qaephar's unstable crust, he had finally bowed to her urgings.

So had begun a series of adventures – more misadventures really. Yet eventually they had found a second Seekstone within some of the ice caves at the base of the mountain. It had taken nearly four weeks before they had found it twinkling like pearl-flecked liquid starlight.

For now, it was a secret only they shared. Kasumi wondered, though, might they be able to use it to make allies with other llorien telepaths? Could the precious ivory crystals do for other llorien telepaths what they did for Vel to the same degree? Or was there some special reason that they affected him in this way? She still could not pretend to understand the crystals' power, but Velamar was helping in that quarter too. Slowly he was beginning to teach her how to use the Seekstones herself. He showed her that even humans had some innate if tiny telepathic ability coded within their genes. Who knew, perhaps one day Kasumi would stare at the Seekstones with the same fondness and intensity which Vel did now.

But not today. Today she was feeling restless. Her nipples pebbled up, so cold. No matter how much kindling Vel plied on the hearth, the fire never seemed to roar hot enough or bright enough. It roared now. Yet still Kasumi felt the chill that was Qaephar, always aware of its icy crust stretching all around the little pocket of warmth they called home.

"Don't be like that," Kasumi purred. "I promise we'll be careful next time. We can go explore some of the shallower caves in the more stable part of the mountain if you prefer."

"The ones which are least likely to have what we're looking for," he groused. "No thank you. I would rather take the risk for real reward than go fruitlessly snooping around and freezing our backsides off while playing it safe. No, you are right, Kasumi. Another expedition is a good idea. Soon, my brave little human. Soon."

Kasumi walked up to him now, her eyes bright. "Have I ever told you how happy you make me?"

Velamar's stubby nose twitched adorably. Meanwhile his stormcloud-gray eyes shone with the vivid intensity of love.

"Not in so many words, no." Saying this, he rose up and slid his nightrobe from his shoulders. He wore nothing underneath.

Kasumi stepped into his arms. She sighed as she felt his hand coax its way between her legs. Two fingers caressed her clitoris. A thrill of pleasure rippled through her core. Even as she felt it, though, she snuck her hand downward and grasped the base of his now engorged cock. Velamar's lips found her breasts and he sucked on her nipples with devotion.

Kasumi's head tipped backward. She let out a long, throaty moan as his lips and fingers eroded her will to resist. Meanwhile she pumped her hand up and down his erection faster and faster. Soon those fingers felt a familiar stickiness – pre-cum presaging pleasure.

"Vel…"

"SSSHHH, my little human. You need to sit on this cock now."

"I know," she agreed, her breath hitching as his fingers continued to cajole her nerve bundle. She almost came on his fingers right then and there.

But he abruptly drew back and sat down on the chair at his desk. He glanced meaningfully at his stiff shaft, rigid as a spear. She climbed onto the chair, her graceful fingers grasping the base of his manhood and positioning it. She positioned the purple-colored tip until it nestled between her labia. Then she sank down. Pure bliss flowed through her as she engulfed him. His shaft, so deeply embedded, sent a coursing need through her entire body as his hands cupped her ass cheeks. They were joined. God, she needed this. Kasumi never tired of this. As she began to pump her body up and down his length, friction and sensation dovetailed together and took them both to new heights. Again and again, Kasumi's cunt slammed down onto him until only his testicles showed beneath her bouncing ass. Velamar's groans, meanwhile, seemed to deepen the more her pussy clamped onto his cock. With loud smacks his palms smote Kasumi's ass cheeks. The resulting sensations spurred the Earth Alliance officer's libido to fresh pinnacles.

A first contact between human and alien had become something much, much more.

Whatever happened, Velamar was hers and she was his. Perhaps the power of the crystals would let them communicate with people in the far flung reaches of space one day. But until that day came, they had each other. Until that day came, they would not wait to start living. They would live day by day, hour by hour, right now. Love too. They would live and love without regret in a present filled with new discoveries each day.

"Velamar! OOOHHH!!" She couldn't hold back.

"Kasumi… AHH!" Neither could he.

The slender woman screamed her lover's name as the orgasm ripped through her, convulsing on his lap. The alien growled a release of his own, his sperm coating his lover's insides like a soothing balm.

~ * ~

Chapter 13
Two Newcomers, One Tiny, One Not So Tiny
~ * ~ * ~ * ~

Three Months Later…

Snow and ice sheathed the six-level home of Velamar and Kasumi, bearing down with incredible weight. Yet still the refuge's framework of zirconen steel held.

Kasumi felt like that zirconen steel now – keeping so much at bay, wondering when or if she might buckle any day now. Any hour. Any minute.

She started panicking. Again.

"I can feel it. It might be coming," she moaned. She clutched her belly, a belly no longer smooth and flat.

Velamar came beside her along the bed. He stroked her face. Her nightshirt, once flowing and several sizes too big, now fit snugly around her midsection. It was also the fifth he had made for her using the matter-resynthesizer in just the past week. Her pregnancy hadn't started to show until just over two months ago – a pregnancy that had astounded and defied all expectations.

"These are phantom contractions, Kasumi. They will pass. It's all right."

"It is *not* all right," she snapped. Pain wormed its way through every vein. Her forehead throbbed. No, her entire *body* throbbed. And this was just over four months into her pregnancy. She had nearly eight months to go!

~ * ~

"I'm going to die," she nearly wailed. The hormonal swings that her interspecies pregnancy brought now hit her with full force.

"Kasumi, I'm right here. I'm not going anywhere. You are going to be all right, I promise you, and so is the baby."

They couldn't give her any pain meds. It might affect the baby. Llorien children were notoriously fragile and they didn't know how much of the baby's physiology had been affected by the DNA of its father. About ten weeks ago, Kasumi had begun to feel 'off.' The foods she normally enjoyed tasted bland or bitter, and foods she normally *hated* became the very ones she craved. Soon after, Velamar and Kasumi had been shocked to discover that she was pregnant.

This wasn't even supposed to be *possible*. All of Velamar's previous companions had been of other species and this had never posed an issue. Llorien procreative compatibility with other alien species was almost nonexistent. Accumulated llorien medical knowledge dating back thousands of years spoke of only *very* rare exceptions. All of the medical texts in Velamar's extensive library confirmed it.

But Velamar was fast learning that there was a vast, *vast* difference between an exceedingly unlikely event and the impossible.

"Breathe with me, Kasumi. Breathe. This will pass. This will pass, I swear to you."

"The baby is going to die. I can feel it." Sweat sheened across her forehead now. The young woman looked at him with a helpless terror that broke Velamar's heart. Velamar had a medical bay on level five with an impressive stock of medicines and the medical sources in Velamar's digital library were considerable. But sometimes there was no substitute for a healer. This was the llorien equivalent of a human doctor and Velamar would have given his right and left arms to have one at their side right now. Instead, he did the next best thing, the only thing he could, really. He used his telepathy to calm her and help ease her pain.

"Kasumi. Look at me." He stroked her hair and kissed her forehead. He cupped her face and joined her mind to his. Not a mind-share. Something else. The power of the three Seekstones they now had

had taught him new ways to control and channel his abilities. He infused her mind with senses of pleasure. These began to crowd out the synapses in her brain shooting signals of pain. He deepened the connection. More telepathic tendrils reached outward. Now he stroked the side of her face and added a soothing auditory stimulus to go along with the pleasure. Kasumi's face softened. Velamar could feel his telepathic inputs reaching the baby now. That was okay. He just had to be careful. He redirected most of the telepathic energy through Kasumi, letting only the residual sensations trickle through to the baby inside her.

You have been so brave, Kasumi, and you are stronger than you know. That's all Velamar could think as he watched Kasumi close her eyes. She lay back, the pain at bay. Her breathing settled into a rhythm again. Soon she drifted toward sleep. He kissed her sweat-slick hair and heaved himself gingerly onto the bed beside her. She shifted, and he cradled her head in his lap. Soon he found his hands caressing her hair. It became a never-ending motion. He continued on like that, his fingers moving and stroking as naturally as breathing.

After a long, long time, she opened her eyes.

"I stink, don't I?"

She was covered in sweat. Her jet-black hair gleamed.

"You do not stink, my little human. You are merely sweaty. There is a difference."

"Not a meaningful one," she griped. She sat up carefully. When he hovered near her like the overprotective mate he was, she shooed him to the side with one hand.

"The contractions are gone. I'm fine. Help me up." He helped her out of bed, then helped her navigate to the shower. Without a word, he helped her take off her sleepshirt. She stepped onto the tiles and turned on the water. Standing beneath the cleansing spray, her naked body seemed to glow. He stared at the swell of her belly and her enlarged breasts and Velamar Azarune decided that there was no miracle greater or more precious in the entire universe than the sight of a mother with child. This was what beauty looked like. A kind of beauty purer than even the beauty of a woman alone because of the fragile budding of new life and what it all meant. This was a future unlooked for – and yet if he could go back, he would do it all again.

"You can join me if you want," she offered. He marveled at her. One moment her hormones had her on the ropes. The next moment she was completely herself again.

"I think I will." Velamar disrobed and stepped into the shower behind her. She turned to kiss him. The spray of the water caressed them both as their tongues mingled, mouths moving in tandem. Kasumi's hair had grown to long, ebon-black tresses which now gleamed as they streamed to the middle of her back. He loved to feel his fingers running through their smooth silkiness, now made heavy from being drenched. Velamar kissed the side of her mouth, then continued to forge a trail of more kisses down the side of her neck all the way to her collar bone. Then he shifted – his tongue lapping at Kasumi's hyper-sensitive nipples. The woman squealed.

"AHH!!! Vel!" she growled reprovingly, but the heat in her eyes said something else. He gently spun her around and had her get down on her hands and knees. The muscular alien knelt behind her. He admired her glistening ass cheeks before nudging his tongue between her labia. She stiffened, then melted beneath his touch as the alien's tongue lapped at her wet pussy. Wet not just from the shower either…

"Ooohhh god… Vel… ohhhh!" Kasumi's body twitched and shuddered with pleasure as he ate her out with fervent focus. The Earth Alliance officer's moans mingled with the soothing spray of the shower. As he thought of the life growing inside her, the llorien's tongue dove with a fury of passion, laving her soft folds with an infinite love. Meanwhile, Kasumi's head remained bowed, her breathing rent by gasps of pleasure, her ass nudging backward as she thrust her pussy against his face.

Giving pleasure to the mother of my child... there is no greater feeling in this world Velamar decided. He redoubled his efforts. His teeth nipped playfully at Kasumi's clit. Then he captured her clit and sucked on it with all his tender might. Kasumi's throbbing nerve bundle released an explosion of sensations and sent it hurtling through her entire body. The young woman trembled, her pussy twitching in the throes of climax, grinding her sex against his mouth as she let out a long, plaintive cry.

"AAAAAHHHHHH!!!!!" Kasumi's body was still trembling when Velamar stood up and fed his cock – harder now than zirconen steel – into his beloved's cunt. He shoved it in slowly but inexorably, savoring the snug squeeze of Kasumi's walls. Kasumi moaned, her head still bowed, her enlarged breasts now tipped with hardened nipples.

"Yes, *yes*. Give me your cock," she begged.

"It's all for you, my little human. Take it," he growled, giving her ass a swat which made her shiver with delight at the sudden sensation. He fucked her like that beneath the hot spray of the shower as time stood still for them. Only their joined bodies mattered anymore. Yet he fucked her gently too, with such care, aware of her fragility and the life inside her needing constant nourishment and protection. They made love like that for a good half hour, his manhood tenderly plowing into Kasumi's body. His cock stroked her core. His hands gathered her hair back as if it were made of jewels. Her moans were the only music he needed. Then he was filling her to the hilt, only his testicles visible as the rush of exquisite pleasure tore the savage growl of release from his throat.

"UGGGHH!!!!"

"Yes! Yes!" Kasumi gasped.

Now Velamar felt his cock twitching, surrendering to the squeeze of his companion's pussy, emptying a load of virile llorien seed deep into his little human's love-hole.

At last, spent and sated, Velamar pulled out of his mate. He helped the woman stand on wobbly legs. The swell of her belly had never looked more breath-taking to him. She gave him a sly grin, her hand straying to the base of his wilting shaft. Grasping him, she looked at him. Her eyes gleamed with a question – more of a request really. A request for an encore.

He was about to offer her just that when the unthinkable happened. The communications array Kasumi had fixed last month now flared to life. The insistent beeping of its alert came all the way from the study. Strident jabs of sound echoed off the walls.

Kasumi stiffened. Shower forgotten, she stepped out dripping wet. Velamar handed her a towel and they both rushed to the study together. Kasumi had set the communications array to detect any local chatter and not to transmit anything for fear of angering the Ilorien authorities. It had seemed quite the forlorn hope, especially given the damaged array's short range. And yet…

"This is Captain Karillion of the *Starship Nightingale*. Is anyone out there? Do you read?"

Velamar and Kasumi exchanged looks of disbelief.

"I repeat, this is Captain Karillion of the human *Starship Nightingale*. This is Captain Karillion of the Galactic Fleet of the Earth Alliance. *Starship Dragonfly*, are you out there?"

Before Velamar could stop her, Kasumi switched the array to transmit mode and responded to their hail.

"*Starship Nightingale*, this is Ensign Kasumi Ogawa of the *Starship Dragonfly*. It's good to hear your voice. Please advise we are on the surface of an icy M-Class planet. I'll transmit you our exact location. Stand by."

Kasumi's fingers glided across the array in a blur of motion.

Velamar had tensed up with worry the moment he'd heard the starship's message. Isolation protocols notwithstanding, the llorien monitoring and defense grid authorities would not dare to start hostilities with a powerful alien warship. That put them in a dicey situation though. If they didn't go with these humans and let the crew of the *Nightingale* evacuate them, there would be hell to pay. Kasumi's action just now had been decisive. There was no going back. The die was cast.

Leaving Qaephar was the only option that made any sense. At least for Kasumi. Which left Velamar with a choice. Stay here and face his punishment while abandoning his wife and child, never to see them ever again… or go with them and become a fugitive.

It hardly seemed a choice at all.

Location sent, Kasumi now sat down and slumped in the chair at Velamar's desk. She looked at him and an apology shone in her eyes.

"Vel, I know I shouldn't have…"

"No, Kas, you did the right thing." Velamar couldn't help feeling a certain pang of regret. He would miss this place, strange as it seemed. What had begun as his prison had become his home.

Tears now filled Kasumi's eyes. She began to sob with relief, and with what Velamar realized had to be joy. It was an infectious joy too. It was a joy which Velamar's telepathic senses chose to savor. Soon those tears of joy flowed down not just her cheeks, but his as well.

"Come with me?" she managed to choke out despite the torrent of emotion.

Velamar nodded. "We're a family, Kasumi. Wherever you go, wherever our child goes, that's where I'll be."

Tears pouring down her cheeks like snowmelt, Kasumi nodded.

"Vel, I love you so much." She surged into his arms. She hugged him tight. Velamar's hands slid along her back as he tucked her head beneath his chin and embraced her like he might never let her go.

Throwing away a comfortable life in exile for this extraordinary woman might just be the smartest thing I've ever done he thought with a sense of oddly rueful gratitude. Still, he had his doubts. He had his fears. The unknown had a way of doing that when confronting a llorien quite set in his ways.

The world, the universe, it hurled surprises and the unknown at a person every single day. But it was worth it. He had a child. Somehow his companion's people had found her. He had no home now perhaps, but in a way, of course, he did. And he always would. After all, home was never really a *place*.

Now, as Velamar nuzzled the silky, jet-black hair of his little human, he marveled at what he had gained in the space of just over seven short months and tried to prepare himself for the journey to come.

~ * ~

Chapter 14
Elixir of Forgetfulness
~ * ~ * ~ * ~

Fourteen Months Later…

The ship's engines hummed as it floated along on thrust-power only, a silver speck in the immensity of space. The llorien prison ship *Vhreng Gar Quan* had no rendezvous planned anytime soon. It sat in orbit around a border moon unhurried and unconcerned. Unlike most llorien prison ships, this one had a science lab and a few other meager amenities for the guards who kept watch and the doctors who studied and gathered their data.

Deep in the belly of the ship, two naked prisoners lived in a rectangular cell of maybe 15 by 20 feet. Kasumi Ogawa and Velamar Azarune had not envisioned this as their future. Fourteen months ago, that future had seemed bright indeed. The *Starship Nightingale* had picked them up and prepared to return to the Anomaly. The overjoyed communications officer and her alien husband had looked forward to starting their family.

But that hope met a vicious end when the llorien Iccutarra Monitoring and Defense Grid (IMDG) forces, in charge of keeping powerful llorien telepaths like Velamar safely imprisoned on their appointed planets of exile, swooped in and attacked the human warship. With awesome ferocity and withering precision, the defense grid ships swarmed and overwhelmed the lone human vessel. Boarding the ship, they fought their way to the bridge, taking full control and killing all who refused to surrender.

Velamar had been helpless to stop them. Helpless to protect his pregnant wife and unborn child.

When they had discovered that Velamar's human mate was indeed pregnant with a half-lorien baby, the llorien authorities were intrigued. Instead of condemning Velamar to execution or making him start over alone on an even harsher planet than Qaephar, they allowed Velamar and Kasumi a kind of mercy, letting them become prisoners together on a prison ship with rudimentary medical facilities. They waited until Kasumi gave birth and then whisked the child away to study.

Now, Velamar and his beloved human were left largely forgotten, assigned to their floating prison in the black. Llorien guards watched and monitored their cell at all times. The bare walls were made of zirconen reinforced cinderblock, and the pitiless warden refused to allow them even the basic amenity of a threadbare blanket.

The prison cell's only two questionable amenities were this then: a wide zirconen steel toilet in the corner and beside it a high-powered overhead shower that sprayed with the harsh velocity of a hose with freezing water at a designated time, for five minutes, once per day.

This was the entirety of their existence: a Spartan, ascetic life filled with monotony except for one thing. They had each other. Despite all that they had been through, Kasumi and Velamar clung to the knowledge that they were still alive and that they were at least together. Somehow the grief at losing their child brought them even closer together still.

Now, as the cycle on the prison ship changed from 'day watch' to 'night watch,' Kasumi and Velamar made do the best they could.

"Please Vel, be with me," Kasumi pleaded.

The naked human had her wrists shackled in front of her. Velamar had the same shackles around his wrists too.

The mottled alien watched as his slender mate got onto her hands and knees, raising her pussy high in the air.

"Please, Vel."

He hardly felt in the mood, but Vel decided he would do it for her. To add insult to injury, though, there were limits on what they could do. The guards did not allow them to have full vaginal intercourse. The llorien authorities had apparently decided that one exotic human-llorien half-breed child was quite enough and did not want the medical complications that might come if Kasumi got pregnant again. As a result, the couple had only one true alternative to achieve the same kind of physical intimacy and closeness.

Velamar's calloused hands slid along the smooth, well-sculpted contours of Kasumi's buttocks. He spit on his right index finger and then spit a copious glob of his llorien saliva into the puckered opening of Kasumi's anus. Kasumi sighed, tensing up as the digit invaded her bottom. As much as her body felt anxious over the invasion to come, she welcomed it. This was the only way that she and Vel could truly be together, be close and become one - well, at least as long as they remained on this hellish prison ship.

"Oh Vel. Yes. Please," she cooed softly. She tried to relax her sphincter muscles as his finger slipped in a little deeper, spreading the saliva-lubricant inside her. Meanwhile, his other hand slipped to her pussy and began to give her clitoris some attention. She bit her bottom lip, closed her eyes, and focused on the exquisite sensations.

Oooohhh. Help me forget. Please, I just want to feel you.

Kasumi's thoughts were interrupted soon after. Just as Velamar went to kneel behind her, the prison ship comms squawked from the ceiling of their cell.

"Remember, Subject 126, penetration of the female's procreation hole for mating purposes is *not* permitted." Ignoring the indignity of that cold, dehumanizing voice, the llorien telepath rested the length of his purple cock across the cleft of Kasumi's ass. He continued to awkwardly reach with his shackled hands underneath to stroke the slender woman's sex. Kasumi bowed her head, her own shackled hands clenched up as she let the soothing euphoria of her throbbing clit distract her from the bleakness of existence.

The anticipation built in Kasumi as she felt that hot, warm shaft, throbbing too just like her pussy, resting against the crack of her ass.

Oooh this is going to hurt, but I want it. It's worth it. She prepared herself. She wanted to feel close to Velamar, and this was the best way among all the less than ideal options. The gorgeous Earth Alliance fleet officer felt her breath catch, her cunt trickling its fluids onto Velamar's fingers.

The llorien telepath pulled his hands away, sucking on her juices. The fragrance of them stoked his senses and provided a poignant comfort despite their situation.

I love you, Kasumi. I am sorry I could not save our child he thought sadly. Living in such a neglected condition in their cell, Vel's telepathic powers had withered and atrophied. He couldn't mind-share with her, much less reach out with his telepathic abilities. His Seekstones had been confiscated along with everything else that had ever been theirs. They had only this, now: only their own bodies.

Now Vel's aroused cock began doing what excited llorien cocks always did: it began to leak a continuous flow of clear-whitish fluid. An inexhaustible supply of alien pre-cum seeped from the tip of that penis into Kasumi's ass. Vel waited until a good amount of the lubricating pre-cum had entered her ass before trying her tightest opening.

The llorien lover pressed the bulbous tip of his manhood at Kasumi's anus. The black-haired beauty groaned and tried to relax her sphincter to let him in, but it was difficult. If Velamar had still retained some of his telepathic powers, he could have made the transition easier for her; as it was, all he could do was thrust very slowly and very gently. The muscular llorien patiently pressed his cock-head into her wrinkled hole while Kasumi clenched her teeth and waited out the discomfort.

"Vel, keep going. Don't stop," she encouraged him, her words belying the tenseness of her body, stiff and trembling as that llorien shaft slowly sank into her too-tight hole.

"Are you sure you can handle this, my little human?" Vel murmured with a mixture of affection and doubt.

"I said do it," Kasumi hissed back. She clenched her shackled hands so hard now that the knuckles stood out like ivory ridges. Forcing herself to relax, she strove mightily to let in the first inch of that impossibly thick llorien spear.

"Kas," Velamar said, a note of warning in his voice, "I don't want to tear you." He was worried that despite the copious lubrication he still would. After all, a llorien cock was not just longer but also thicker than an average human's. But Kasumi through clenched teeth held on. She focused on her breathing and even managed to gently press her bottom backward to meet the mounting pressure of Velamar's tip.

Then she felt it. The point of that fleshy spear found its way past her sphincter. With a sudden lurch, she felt something give, felt an incredible sensation of fullness as the first two to three inches of llorien cock seated itself between her ass cheeks.

"AHHH!!!!"

"You're doing great, Kas," Velamar cooed, encouraging his mate. He didn't thrust yet. Not yet. He knew it would be dangerous to try. He just held himself still, the two to three inches embedded in her bottom, letting the human's fragile, distended anus slowly acclimate. And all the while he caressed the woman's butt cheeks and told her how beautiful she was, how much he loved her.

Now, very tenderly, llorien reached out and gathered up the long, ebon tresses of Kasumi's hair. In captivity the linguist officer's hair had grown long indeed. It flowed down her back like a midnight waterfall, ending almost at her tailbone. He wrapped it in his fist for leverage and slowly pulled his wrist back.

As Kasumi's head tipped upward, she felt Vel's cock slide out and back in. Out and back in. Out… and back *in*. The three inches in and out offered searing sensation, a closeness that felt like a cross between sandpaper and a very rough cone sliding deep inside her. The apparent contradiction of it, the conflicting sensations, was hard to put into anything coherent. The groan that escaped her lips came out tinged with a husky note of pleasure.

Kasumi felt the bite of her hair pulling at her scalp and welcomed it; Vel knew she liked this, to have her hair tugged during intercourse. Now he leaned in on that, pulling her hair more sharply and venturing to thrust more deeply. His pre-cum oozing shaft had now had plenty of time to lubricate her anus, turning it into a viscous mess. He pulled in and out harder now, faster, five inches lancing her bottom, then six.

"Vel!" Kasumi crooned. "Fuck me, my love. FUCK ME." She closed her eyes and relished the sensation of him ravaging her, of her anus taking that big llorien cock. She let her demons fall away as intimacy and love for her mate replaced all the dread and despair of each new day. Kasumi felt her nipples pebble up with surging libido, those brown tips hard and burning to be touched. Velamar would have touched them if he could have. Yearned to touch them. Yet his shackled hands instead temporarily released her hair only to firmly plant themselves on her ass, spreading her cheeks wider as he slammed his vein-engorged manhood deep into that tiny human asshole.

"Uhhh!!! UHH!!!!" Velamar ground out. His hips moved back and forth in a flurry now. His heavy llorien balls smacked gently against her smooth ass cheeks as his penis stretched and anally deflowered her.

Meanwhile Kasumi felt a delirium building up inside of her. The shared membrane between her pussy and ass felt as if it was on fire, with the friction of Vel's cock sawing in and out, back and forth, hard in and out with wet sounds of suction.

Pound my ass. Yessss... Vel, I love you. No matter what happens, we're together and that's all that matters. I want to FEEL you inside me. Mmmm. Make me forget. Make me forget everything but how much you care for me, how much you love me. You mean everything to me. You're the tether, the tenuous thread of sanity that keeps me going…

Even as these thoughts swam through her brain and settled like a balm on the tattered remnants of her shattered soul, Kasumi felt herself lose control. The black-haired female cried out, her breasts jiggling wildly as she arched her back, bucking backward against Vel's thrusting cock in the throes of climax.

"AAAAAAYYYYYY!!!!! YAAAAAAA!" Kasumi screeched, her pussy clamping up around a cock that wasn't there, gushing fluids even as she felt the sting of her hair yanked back from her scalp, a sting that made her feel truly alive and oddly enhanced every sensation.

Velamar looked down critically. The llorien telepath saw the tiniest trace of red streak his pre-cum coated member. Apparently he had torn her a bit despite trying to be careful. Yet between all the euphoria and the adrenaline, Kasumi didn't seem to notice. She just kept panting and begging for more, pushing her anus back against his pummeling shaft. She was milking his balls, making it impossible not to surrender.

The musclebound llorien watched his penis vanish between those finely sculpted ass cheeks. He leaned over her now, gripping her shoulders, using the leverage of his position above and behind her to really rail her from behind.

"Oh god! Vel! DON'T STOP!!!" Kasumi squealed. A second orgasm rushed up to overshadow the power of the first. Kasumi's clitoris stiffened in ecstasy and surrendered in what might as well have been a shower of sparks. The naked female crooned and squealed even louder. Her eyes snapped open as she looked up at the ceiling, and then it happened.

Velamar felt his cock crash downward with finality, impaling his little human's overstretched ass. Then he felt the seed pumping into her, shooting forth from the tip of his purple penis like a Nurmenzian stallion's organ brought to the finish line in the midst of mating.

Blast after blast, wave after wave of the telepath's jism exploded in Kasumi's bottom. So powerful were the jets bursting from Vel's cock that the excess quickly formed a backflow.

The spent llorien pulled out with a grunt and watched as the heavy stream of seed - a vivid deep purple because it had been so long since Velamar had emptied his balls - oozed down the crack of her ass all the way to her pussy.

"Do not let your child-making fluids get inside her procreation hole," a warning voice called over the prison's comm system. Vel quickly knelt and stuck his tongue out, catching his own seed as it slid down his lover's ass.

Finally, lapping up the last of the mess he'd made, or so it seemed, he turned Kasumi around. Her dazed look told him everything he needed to know.

I needed this, Vel. Thank you.

"My big sexy alien," she murmured, giving him a wan smile as her breathing began to recover. "Thank you. Thank you for being willing to comfort me in the way I needed."

Now that he'd spent himself, he was prepared to pull her to him, to cuddle with her on the cold cinderblock floor and cushion her body above his to keep her warm, but she stopped him. She put her shackled hands against his chest to push him back.

"No. Wait. Not yet." Laying down below him face-up while he knelt there, she began to lap at his just-emptied testicles. Meanwhile, her shackled hands began to rub and pump the base of his cock. It wasn't long before a new stirring began deep within his loins. A fresh clear-whitish avalanche of fluids slid down the sides of his cock even as Kasumi's delicate face lay smothered beneath the folds of his balls. He could hear her muffled slurps beneath him.

"SLRP!! *Mmm*!!!! SLRP!!"

"Kasumi," he warned, libido reawakening in him like a cosmic phoenix.

But meanwhile, he looked down and noticed the reddish cum trickling from his beloved's ravaged asshole. Kasumi's distended anus still hadn't recovered to its former size, the gaping hole quivering from the passionate pounding it had received.

Kasumi didn't care though. She and her alien soulmate were together. Even in this hell of a prison, they would survive. They would help each other get through this one day, one cycle at a time.

"Kas! UGHHH!!!"

Velamar groaned as if his next breath might be his last, a second batch of seed fountaining in a wide spray that covered his little human's chest and belly.

Kasumi, you didn't deserve this fate. I hope that one day, somehow, we will be a family again. Oh, if only we could know, what has happened to our child???

The unknown fate of their child haunted him, but for the moment he could dwell in the welcoming abyss of post-coitus forgetfulness. He sighed as he watched his little human kneeling before him, her breasts glistening with his cum, licking the tip of his twice-sated cock as if she could slurp up an elixir from it to grant a more permanent forgetfulness. Pushing her onto her back, he knelt between his little human's legs and began to lap up the coppery tang and llorien sperm seeping from the ruined ass of the woman he loved.

~ * ~

~ * ~

Chapter 15
A Dangerous Gift
~ * ~ * ~ * ~

Kasumi and Velamar's routine on the *Vhreng Gar Quan* proved to be reliable if nothing else. Once per day, the llorien prison guards dropped their food through a grate in the ceiling. It had the consistency of fresh, creamy mashed potatoes of Earth, with a color akin to pumpkin-orange. To defy the monotony, sometimes the human and her alien lover would have a food fight together, laughing and chasing each other with handfuls of the 'xlamdur.'

As for the weekly routine, that was not something Kasumi looked forward to exactly - and this morning cycle was no different.

Now, as the cell door slid open with something between a whisper and a hiss, six llorien defense grid guards stomped into the room.

"Weekly grooming for the female," one guard barked tersely. A table was wheeled in. The lead guard, a llorien with black, diamond-shaped mottles across his forehead, Kasumi had helpfully nicknamed 'Black Diamond.'

Black Diamond proceeded to scrub Kasumi down with a sanitizing gel-pad that had a soft, sponge-like coating on one side which secreted body wash and a harsher, bristled back to abrasively remove dead skin and grime. Next, he trimmed her nails. Then he brushed out her hair. This was done efficiently almost to the point of roughly. As to why they didn't simply let the prisoners see to their own hygiene, Velamar had explained to his wife that the warden did not trust prisoners to be left unsupervised with even a single item in case they created something from even the most mundane object to be a weapon or tool of escape. *No wonder we are allowed only our own bodies* Kasumi had thought glumly. *The warden here is a paranoid sadist.* Then again, maybe the paranoia was justified. Kasumi sometimes wondered who else the lloriens might be keeping on the prison ship.

Fortunately, though, Kasumi had learned to tolerate these intrusive, weekly humiliations with surprising aplomb. Though Black Diamond and the guards were always terse and gruff, not even willing to share their names, Kasumi spoke to her handlers with easy familiarity by now. Over the course of fourteen months, she had long lost any concerns about modesty and just learned to embrace humor to make the best of things.

Today would be no different...

"Beautiful day, isn't it? Look at those stars. They're shining even brighter than usual," Kasumi quipped as Black Diamond ushered two llorien guards forward. The 'bed' they'd wheeled in was really just a horizontal metal slab.

"You know what must be done," Black Diamond grumbled. "Now cooperate."

The naked woman leapt onto the aliens' gurney and lay down face up.

"Raise your arms." Kasumi did and Black Diamond drew out his shaving tool. Firsts he applied a frothy lubricant to her armpits, shaving each. Then he did the same to the front of each leg. "Lift your leg, please. Now the other." She complied as he finished making each of her legs smoother than silk.

"So," Kasumi broached with the best conversational voice she could muster, "any chance we could have dessert today? You know, just to change things up a bit?"

No matter what she said, their llorien minders never did answer her. Black Diamond remained his usual tight-lipped self.

Once he had finished with her legs, it came time to do the final, most intimate aspect of her hygiene-regimen. Kasumi had initially dreaded this with heart-pounding anxiety, but as with every other aspect of her existence here on the ship, she'd learned to adapt.

"Spread your legs."

Once again, the black-haired human complied. She felt the soft spray of foam cover her sex. The alien lathered it across her pubic hair before applying the razor. Kasumi closed her eyes as the alien shaved her sex with precise, dehumanizing swipes. Even though Velamar's telepath abilities were so atrophied as to be almost dormant, every time this happened she could sense his outrage. She tried to be calm not just for her own sake but for his too. Each time the razor shorn away the hair to leave the skin around her pussy perfectly smooth, Kasumi sent her mind wandering to better places. Meanwhile, Black Diamond attended to the woman's cunt as if he was a mechanic from old Earth changing the oil of a car.

Once he had finished, he didn't even say a word. Black Diamond simply loaded up the hygiene-related tools in a large clear bag, handed it to one of the guards, and turned to leave. The other five guards wheeled the gurney out and shut the cell behind them.

It would be Velamar's turn to be groomed another day: why they didn't arrange to do both prisoners at once, only the guards or the warden knew.

Now, with the weekly ordeal over, Kasumi ran into Vel's arms.

"I've got you," he whispered. His arms encircled her protectively. She inhaled his scent for comfort. His strength gave her strength. Her nipples pressed against the planes of his chest, against muscles that were the only walls capable of protecting her in this dreary place.

"Next time you should tell them some jokes. Maybe some llorien puns? I'll teach you a few."

Kasumi drew back and looked up at the man she loved. She even managed a tiny grin. "I would like that very much." Vel leaned down and kissed her.

"Want to…?" She let the question hang suggestively in the air.

Velamar frowned. His mottled face darkened. "You have still not fully healed from our last coupling, little human. That… tighter hole is pleasurable for me, do not misunderstand, and I do cherish such intimacy with you, but it was not a hole designed for such a purpose, strictly speaking, or evolved to be used in such a way. Is that not correct?"

"Do you really have to be such a killjoy?" Kasumi rolled her eyes, stepped back, and put both her hands on her hips.

But Velamar's nostrils widened and he picked her up before turning her upside down.

"You want joy, little human? I will give you joy," he growled playfully.

His mouth took her pussy, and from there Kasumi's protests deteriorated into a series of moans, pleas, and - as things progressed - outright squeals. Finally, he set her down panting, and the memory of the weekly grooming session seemed a distant thing.

Just when Vel and she were about to do their daily exercises together though, helping each other stay fit, the whisper-hiss of their cell door intervened.

~ * ~

In walked... Black Diamond. He had returned with his five fellow prison guards. The truth was, Kasumi had come up with a nickname for each of them to amuse herself in her extensive spare time. In each case, she had named them based on their most prominent facial feature, whether that involved the color of the pigment on their mottled facial ridges or some other prominent aspect of their facial structure. Black Diamond was now joined by Red Mottle, Blue Mottle, Mountain Nose, Sharp Eyes, and Wide Brow.

"We have brought you a gift, female."

Kasumi's jaw dropped. Velamar looked on, intrigued. *Wait? Is he actually speaking to me as if I'm a human being?*

"Before we show you, we must secure Subject 126. The telepath is a threat I will not tolerate."

What? The shackles on our wrists aren't enough? Kasumi and Velamar thought almost simultaneously.

Black Diamond nodded at Blue Mottle and Red Mottle. The two llorien guards, one shorter, one taller, took Velamar aside and pressed an invisible panel in the wall. A keypad of sorts thrust out from a secret compartment. Typing in a blur of numbers, Red Mottle made a horizontal bar connected to a chain appear from an opening in the ceiling and lower until the bar was within his reach. Connected to each end of the bar were manacles not unlike the shackles currently confining both captives' wrists.

Blue Mottle proceeded to unlock Velamar's shackles, only to re-shackle them to either side of the suspended bar. Velamar now stood there, stationary in his new shackles.

"You will stay there," Black Diamond intoned. Now he gestured at Wide Brow, Sharp Eyes, and Mountain Nose. The three lloriens withdrew and returned with a hump-shaped base between them, which they set on the floor. From that hump-shaped base protruded a long phallic object. It looked like living tissue, a deep blue with veins of silver and gold. The silver veins along the phallus seemed to glitter while the gold veins almost glowed.

"This llorien manhood is a replica of the warden's own member. He has chosen for us to present it as a gift to you, female."

Kasumi gave him a startled look. Her shock deepened. What was she supposed to say to *that*? The lead prison guard continued.

"It has been enhanced with a substance discovered on a new world brought into the fold of llorien colonization. The silver and gold veins are the result of this injected substance. These devices are currently popular among our own females for the effect they have: they bring… great pleasure." Black Diamond seemed to be studying her, gauging Kasumi's reaction. The lithe and beautiful Earth

Alliance officer tried to school her features, to keep them completely neutral.

"I see. Please tell the warden 'thank you' for me." *It could be fun to use* Kasumi thought. *I bet Vel will have fun finding ways to incorporate it in some of our lovemaking. Besides, my pussy is feeling a little neglected in the cock department* she thought wryly.

Black Diamond shook his head and gestured at it though.

"The warden requires more than a 'thank you.' To prove that you are appreciative of the gift, you must use it."

There was an awkward pause. Velamar's nostrils flared. Kasumi didn't understand at first.

"You mean *now*?"

Black Diamond nodded. "Yes, female. The choice is yours. If not, I can return it and tell the warden you rejected his gift. The decision is up to you."

Kasumi bit her bottom lip. She had no desire to insult their prison warden. He was paranoid and aloof enough as is. Now that he'd made a friendly gesture toward them, wasn't it wise to take him up on it? Even though she'd been Vel's wife for over two years, she still hadn't learned all of the many layers of llorien customs or some of the more esoteric ones - not to mention regional differences between the llorien of various planets throughout their home system. So wisdom to her right now seemed to call for rolling with the punches. Why not? And besides, it could be fun.

It's not like Vel and I haven't had sex in a vid-monitored prison cell for the last fourteen months anyway.

She darted a look toward Vel, who seemed content to let her decide.

"OK. I'll give it a try," she said, blushing bright scarlet. Now, she approached the phallus. It had to be a good 11 inches long, curved, and it was thick too. She leaned down with her shackled hands to grasp the base of it. It was cold to the touch. Ice-cold.

Hmm. Not sure I'm gonna like this she thought, somewhat regretting her decision already.

Black Diamond and the others seemed to sense her hesitation.

"Have you changed your mind, female?"

"No," she said, her nerve steadying. "And please, call me *Kasumi.*"

"As you are my prisoner, I cannot use your name, female. Though perhaps other shorthand names can be arranged."

Oh, for the love of...

"OK, well, I'm ready. You can leave now."

But to her surprise, Black Diamond shook his head. "No, we are ordered to stay. Either you use it now or you don't, and we take it back. We have our orders. We stay to verify your acceptance of the warden's gift."

Their llorien minders were nothing if not didactic. Kasumi sighed. She could see Velamar frowning in the corner of her vision, but her husband said nothing. He knew, like she did, that sometimes custom and proper etiquette had to take precedence over comfort.

OK, let's get on with it.

Kasumi approached the vein-covered shaft and prepared to mount it. To do so, first she wet her fingers and reached down to her pussy. Rubbing herself for a few minutes, she moistened herself up considerably, waiting for arousal to awaken in her. Only when her nipples were hardened into stiff little brown points did Kasumi venture to straddle the hump and position her cunt lips at the bulbous tip of the cock. Then, with ginger care, she slid just the head within her lips and gauged the feel of it. As her pussy engulfed the first inch or two, a deep cold stabbed through her being. She stiffened.

Yet the cold vanished as quickly as it had come. As she continued to lower herself, the slender woman found that the phallus warmed inside her, as if responding to her touch. She placed her shackled hands, palms flat, before her and began to rise up and down, humping the veined manhood.

At first the pleasurable sensations were as she'd expected. Her snug sex felt every inch of that deliciously firm rod inside her. She looked at Velamar and saw the stiff hard-on sticking up unapologetically between his legs.

You like the show, don't you, my big, sweet, sexy ox?

This wasn't as difficult as she'd feared. Soon she forgot about the guards and focused just on her husband and her pleasure. Rising and falling. Lifting and impaling her pussy, she soon felt her wetness coating the phallus. Her cunt juice made the shaft glisten in the light, and the slippery squelch-sounds of a well-lubricated pussy suctioning up the artificial penis soon echoed through the cell.

"Ooohhhh!"

Is that MY voice? Something didn't seem right. Something didn't feel right. The pleasure had reached euphoric levels, but she still hadn't come. To the contrary, all she seemed to want was *more*. Her clit had warmed and stiffened, throbbing with arousal, and yet something else seemed to have entered her veins. A hunger. A hunger that seemed far beyond human.

What's… what's this thing doing to me? Kasumi wondered. Part of her didn't care, though, and the part of her that did was still more than willing to bow to curiosity, to take this sexual adventure and see where it might lead.

When in Rome, do as the Romans… Aaahhhh!!!

Her pussy now felt like it was on fire. Kasumi felt as if she was burning up. The heat of desire coiled through her like a drug, her nipples painfully erect, her breasts aching to be not just touched but mauled. She had never felt hornier in her entire life. Her cunt juices now flooded down the veined manhood. A waterfall of her fluids gushed obscenely. She was coming hard right now and yet… yet that sense of post-orgasm satisfaction eluded her. Kasumi found her clit still throbbing, her body no more sated than before. She found her hands clenching in front of her. She found herself slamming her sex down harder, so hard her teeth rattled.

Deeper. I need it deeper.

"What's happening to me?" she blurted.

"What have you done to her?" Velamar joined in with a mixture of anxiety and disapproval.

Kasumi felt a hand close around her shoulder from behind. She looked up to see Black Diamond addressing her husband.

"There is no need for concern, Subject 126. The female is merely responding to the bliss-substance inserted into the manhood-sculpture. This newly discovered substance ramps up female libido, triggering a surge of hormones and other chemical responses - and apparently works as well on human females as on our own species," Black Diamond added.

"Yes," Kasumi moaned. She awkwardly reached one of her shackled hands between her legs and began to finger her clitoris as she rode the veined shaft. Balancing herself completely on just the other shackled hand proved difficult but not impossible. The dazed look of pleasure in her eyes was complete now, and Kasumi just wanted one thing: more of that cock, and deeper.

"It seems she approves of her gift," Black Diamond said to the llorien males around her. As if that was a sign, as if on cue, all six of the llorien guards began to shrug out of their uniforms. Soon all six stood naked, their own shafts, like Velamar's, erect and engorged.

"What are you doing?" Velamar demanded.

"Nothing that your female does not desire," Black Diamond replied evenly. As the leader of the group, he seemed the one controlling the pace of the action. Now he strode a slow circuit around to the front of Kasumi, blocking her husband from her field of vision. His cock stood out, a purplish pole with steel-silken power. Clear-whitish fluid leaked from the tip, dribbling down the underside like melting water from an Earth glacier in summer.

"Would you like to suck me, human?"

She lunged for his shaft, but he shifted at the last moment, presenting his testicles instead.

"Suck the balls, little cunt." Kasumi groaned with disappointment but took one of his big, cum-filled testicles between her lips. Sucking fervently, she looked up at the cock resting on her forehead. She respositioned both shackled hands in front of her; soon the seal of her cunt lips was sliding fully down the sculpture-cock until the head jolted her cervix. She moaned and kept her lips glued to Black Diamond's balls even as Black Diamond's shaft dribbled a steady trickle of pre-cum into her now damp, sticky hair.

"What do you think, Subject 126? Is your wife horny enough? Would you like to see us all fuck her? Would that please you, to see us all give your human mate such pleasure?"

The words were thrown like daggers, and the prison guard leader didn't bother to turn around to see Velamar's predictable reaction. The telepath saw in only one color right now as he glared at Black Diamond: *red*.

"All right, little cunt, you may now switch to my--"

Before he could even finish getting the words out, though, Kasumi was sucking the tip of his penis like a lollipop. She vacuumed at the pinnacle of his manhood powerfully, putting every ounce of effort into it, filling her lungs and using all the energy she could.

Black Diamond looked over his shoulder at Velamar, whose outrage had only grown.

"See, your wife enjoys the taste of another cock. Is it not beautiful?"

Velamar could only see his wife's bouncing pussy riding the base of the phallus and the sounds of her loud slurping on the other side of the llorien guard now blocking his view.

"SSSSLURRRRP!!!! MMMMM!!!! SLRP!! GLLGGG!!! UGHHH!!! MMM!!! SLRP!! SLRP!"

Black Diamond rested his hand gently on her bobbing head. Her black-as-night hair streamed wildly down her back as she bent to her task. Another orgasm tore through her, and her moan deepened even with a cock-filled throat.

Now Black Diamond couldn't hold back. He groaned, holding the back of her skull, introducing her nose to his pubic curls, shooting potent blasts of hot, lumpy llorien sperm into the back of Kasumi's throat. The naked woman choked and coughed, swallowing what she could before excess streams of it oozed down her chin and fell in great messy swaths onto her breasts.

"AHH. Who's next? I think she'd had enough of the cock-sculpture. Let's give her something warmer and more alive!"

Red Mottle stepped up and lifted the startled woman clear of the artificial phallus. Kasumi felt a brief flash of disappointment on the verge of agony, that feeling of an empty pussy driving her crazy, before Red Mottle bent her over and lanced her cunt from behind.

The dark-haired beauty clenched up her shackled hands and rammed back her sex to meet those pulverizing thrusts.

"Yes, please fuck me! Fuck me! Fuck me!!! FUCK ME!" she shouted. "I need your cock. I need it harder."

A sated Black Diamond meanwhile walked up to Velamar and stood beside him, enjoying the spectacle.

"You see?" the corrupt llorien guard whispered in Velamar's ear. "This bliss-substance, that which our scientists are now calling 'xenadria-6,' is a compound that destroys inhibitions, raises libido, and allows a female to fully embrace their sexual identity on a new level. Just as your sweet human is doing now. Is it not breath-taking. Is it not… magnificent?"

Just as Black Diamond finished twisting the knife, Red Mottle gave Kasumi's ass a mighty slap and came with a devastating shout. Kasumi squealed as she felt herself filled, then looked over her shoulder in dismay as the musclebound llorien pulled out and withdrew.

No sooner had he disappeared, though, another took his place. Sharp Eyes forcibly picked her up, turned her around, and impaled her on his vein-engorged manhood. Kasumi wrapped her arms and legs around him, clinging to him for dear life. Her pussy bounced violently up and down, the llorien's whitish-clear pre-cum sliding free of the seal of the woman's cunt lips all the way down to his large, bouncing testicles.

"Kiss me, you shameless female. Let me feel your lips," Sharp Eyes barked. Kasumi moaned against his mouth, their tongues tussling as Sharp Eyes' cock stretched that tight human pussy.

"Kasumi, please," Velamar called out. "Come back to yourself."

"She can't hear you," Black Diamond growled. "She knows what she was made for: a female is a female, no matter what species. She was made to be *penetrated*, to be loved and loved *hard* by males."

"But I thought…" Velamar sputtered. "She is not to be impregnated. That is the prison's own policy! Is that not what the defense gird leadership has decided?"

Black Diamond nodded with a gaze that glittered. "That may be, but accidents do happen. We can always blame *you*." The llorien laughed. As the laughter died down, the two llorien males could hear the resumption of Kasumi's moans and see Sharp Eyes' balls now coated completely in the fluids trickling from Kasumi's pussy, as well as the pre-cum from Sharp Eyes' own excited cock.

"It appears that your human does not need you as much as you think," Black Diamond observed. "He impales your wife like a champion. I wonder if she will bear his child?"

Velamar watched in disbelief as Sharp Eyes' guttural cry flew through the prison cell. Vel could imagine the millions of llorien sperm rocketing up his wife's pussy, filling her cunt and then some with an army of potent and virile swimmers.

"Mmmm." Black Diamond now watched as Sharp Eyes handed the delirious female to the next man. Blue Mottle took her and impaled her just as Sharp Eyes had done. But instead of standing still and fucking her, he walked over to stand before the chained-up telepath.

"Join in, my friend. Your wife has plenty of holes for all," the llorien guard said mockingly.

Velamar's face darkened, but he saw his wife fully enjoying herself, and what was more, his own balls ached with need, his own shaft ramrod stiff and eager.

"Take her other hole," Black Diamond coaxed. "Did you not enjoy taking it not long ago? Embrace it. Embrace your wife's true self. This is the female within her. The one who craves to be taken."

Biting his lip, Velamar turned away and tried to resist. Deep down, though, he wanted this. Deep down he saw his beautiful wife getting fucked hard and couldn't help but see a kind of hot, erotic symmetry to the entire scene, appalling as it was. So despite his best judgment - resisting every voice inside of him screaming NO! - Velamar groaned and allowed Blue Mottle to press his wife's rosebud opening down against the tip of his cock.

Kasumi's moans and coos suddenly morphed into a shriek of surprise as she felt something against her backdoor. Then the human was instinctively tensing up her sphincter muscle, keeping out the foreign invader.

"Open up for him, pussy. Do it," Blue Mottle growled, grabbing her by the hair and yanking until she looked at him. When she still looked at him blankly, he gave her cheek a gentle but firm slap once, then twice. With her still slow to respond, he reached down and pinched one of her nipples. She yelped. "Answer me!"

"Ayy!!! Oooh but I'm sore there," she half-protested, eyes heavy-lidded with lust.

"Let. Him. In." Blue Mottle's voice brooked no argument, and Kasumi relented. She clenched her eyes shut and tried to relax. A moment later, she felt her husband's cock swamp her defenses, overpower her sphincter's resistance. A massive llorien penis slammed up into her anus. For the first time in her life, the beautiful young linguist had alien cocks double-penetrating her.

Kasumi instantly came, her cunt convulsing, her entire body shaking.

"YES!!!! OH FUCK!!!! I'M GOING TO DIE FROM COMING!!!! PLEASE!!!!!" she crooned, her squeals sailing through the air as her overtaxed body didn't know how to handle the onslaught of stimulation. Her shackled hands gripped the back of Blue Mottle's neck as she kissed him hard.

Meanwhile Vel felt something give way in Kasumi's ass. An extra layer of fluid trickled down his shaft, mingling with his own pre-cum. *She'll need rest after this* he thought. *Her body was not meant to take so much.*

But, hating himself a little, he watched his manhood vanishing between his wife's shapely ass cheeks. He savored the sight of that tight hole stretched to the max impaled on his throbbing member. Soon after, Vel heard Sharp Eyes growl out in climax. He grasped Kasumi by the nape of the neck and shoved her face against his shoulder hard, keeping it tucked beneath his chin while thick ropes of llorien sperm swam up her human love-hole. The moment of his fellow male's ejaculation helped send Velamar over the edge. He groaned and emptied a huge sticky salvo into his wife's bottom. Wave after wave of cum surged into the despoiled ass of the woman he loved.

With exhaustion, Velamar watched his flaccid manhood slip out. It was followed by a heavy stream of red-tinted cum. Vel stared at the distended opening of his wife's ass. Within her bowels lay a reservoir of congealed alien seed, the webbing of her ass stretched taut by a cock far bigger than anything it was meant to handle.

My poor little human…

Next Sharp Eyes handed her into the arms of Mountain Nose. The Ilorien guard, so named for his prominent snout-like appendage, put her back in the doggy-style position. He slid his eager shaft between her raw-rubbed cunt lips and gave her pussy long, deep strokes. Her chest still covered with half-congealed cum, bits of sperm dripping from her to the floor, all Kasumi could do was stare forward in a lust-enshrouded fog, her body screaming for more, her pussy yearning for harder and deeper cock.

"Does this pussy belong to me, female? Hmm? What do you say?" Mountain Nose groaned as he watched his testicles slap against the backs of the woman's thighs.

"It belongs to you. Just fuck me," she panted. "Please don't ever leave my pussy be. It needs to be filled. Oh god, oh yes, oh *please* fill it. Just fill it!! Ooooohhhhh I'm going… oh *yessssss*!"

Kasumi came hard again, but this time something had changed. The chemical spike and euphoria triggered by the substance-infused phallus sculpture was finally starting to wear off. With the sudden nosedive came exhaustion. The gorgeous woman found herself sprawling forward, trembling, her limbs turned to jelly.

"Please…"

Mountain Nose grabbed her by the hair, jerking her face upward. Then he reached around with his free hand, grabbing and squeezing one of her breasts like a stress ball.

"Beg, human. I want to hear you *beg*."

"Please come," she yelped. His hand slid to the front of her neck, gripping her there as he plowed into her with a thrust so violent both their bodies rocked forward, another huge load deposited inside the human-turned-cock-sleeve. Pulling out now, Mountain Nose gave each of the female's ass cheeks an affectionate slap, which made fresh whitish seed ooze out.

"Please…"

One more cock awaited her. Wide Brow approached now. He flipped her onto her back and blanketed his body atop hers. In one smooth motion he slid his entire cock into the wet, willing depths of that human pussy as if it would always be his. He looked up at Velamar.

"Watch your wife get fucked, telepath. Watch me give it to her harder than you ever have," the guard growled with glee.

Velamar heard every one of Kasumi's whimpers, cries, and squeals of rapture as the prison guard fucked her deep. The telepath could only stare with a guilty erection re-forming as he watched his wife's pussy thoroughly despoiled. As he heard Kasumi's tiny shouts and moans, her 'Uuuhs!' and half-broken croaks of 'Y-yes fuck me more' diluted with the occasional 'Please I'm so tired' or even 'Please be gentle, it's sore. My pussy hurts.' Yet the pleasure lashed them both on, female and male alike. Kasumi's shackled hands spread, palms flat, against the chest of the llorien pounding her from above. She looked up at him, whimpering, the friction in her cunt driving her wild as she spread her thighs as wide for him as she could. Now her eyes met his in the moment he growled out the pinnacle of his existence and flooded her with the fiery heat of a few million sperm.

At last, he pulled out, and Velamar thought that it might finally, mercifully, be over.

But it wasn't. Not quite.

Black Diamond had re-hardened. Now he swiveled Kasumi around so that as she lay there Vel could see the excess jism leaking out of her thoroughly used sex. The oozing sludge of llorien spunk pooled on the floor between her thighs. Then Black Diamond was lowering himself, inserting his shaft inside the wet-and-sloppy paradise. His shaft split her silken folds. Even with her cunt stuffed now, though, more seed oozed from her loosened asshole.

"You see that?" Sharp Eyes said, and the other guards, all sated, came up to tease Velamar too. "Your wife is our shameless-soaked cum-dump and she's LOVING it. Have you ever taken her so thoroughly before? Exhausted the limits of her endurance as we have?"

Velamar knew the truth of it.

No. No I have not. He felt a strange mixture of shame, regret, but also fierce delight. He didn't understand it, but part of him felt proud... actually *proud* that his wife had successfully taken this many llorien cocks and would live to tell of it. Vel watched now as Black Diamond's manhood drove like a hammer between Kasumi's cunt lips. Wet sounds echoed in the cell.

SPLORT!!! SPLAT!!! SPLORT!!!!

Kasumi's moans were drifting toward yet another almost cruelly intense orgasm. Her body couldn't take much more of this. At last she shuddered, passing out from the intensity of the pleasure.

Meanwhile, Black Diamond continued his tireless thrusting. Velamar stared at the llorien guard's ass cheeks clenched up with effort, then heard the loudest shout of the night. Black Diamond's testicles shot forward and a moment later his member exploded with a thick, viscous, baby-making geyser inside that already cum-drenched human pussy.

"AAAAHHHHHH!!!!!"

It took what seemed like an eternity for Black Diamond to empty the last of the churning seed from his llorien testicles. When he pulled out, he stared at the unconscious human female with affection. He gave her pussy an affectionate swat which sounded with a loud *SPLAT* as more cum trickled out of her.

"We fucked your wife well for you, telepath. She will never forget it." Black Diamond nodded toward the sculpture. "If you wish to have her fuck you with the eagerness of a wild hrak'narii in heat, have her use that and, as you can see, you will not be disappointed!"

~ * ~

Later… much later, Kasumi awoke nestled in Velamar's arms. Her entire body ached, inside and out. Her pussy felt like it had been fucked constantly for days. Her mouth felt dry. Her nipples throbbed. Even her clitoris felt like a successive parade of one hundred lovers had nipped playfully at it and sucked that engorged nub to oblivion.

"Vel," she croaked, her eyes fluttering. "Did…" She didn't know what to say. "Did that really happen?"

Instead of replying though, he merely kissed her brow. "You were magnificent, my little human. You have nothing to be ashamed of." He paused, as if uncertain whether to tell her something. "I had the guards take away that… device. It gave you great pleasure, but I worry for your welfare. It removes all inhibitions, but inhibitions exist for a reason and I feared you would… hurt yourself if you abandoned yourself to the effects of whatever 'substance' they inserted inside that thing."

Kasumi groggily opened her eyes as memory came flooding back. Of the giant phallus gleaming with veins of gold and silver like the gossamer threads of something otherworldly. Of humping the artificial shaft and feeling indescribable euphoria.

"It was more curse than blessing," she confessed. "As much as it made me feel joy in the moment, it wasn't *real* joy. It was… a shortcut to joy. It…"

Velamar stroked her hair, looked patiently into her eyes with love and tenderness, and waited for her to continue.

"It was a joy that robbed me of *me*. I could lose myself in it, but that was just it. I *lost* myself. I couldn't think, I couldn't appreciate what was happening to me. The quiet love you and I share, that deeper connection, was absent, replaced by just an, I don't know, a chemical-joy, a present-only kind of pleasure that feels empty afterward." Kasumi reached out and stroked Velamar's cheek. "No matter how hard they fucked me, no matter what half-intelligible encouragement I may have squealed, it wasn't you, Vel. I love *you*. I only want to be with *you*. The guards - all they could do was *fuck me*. You, Vel, *make love* to me.

Velamar kissed his favorite human on the lips with a soft, tender, care that lingered long after their mouths drifted apart.

"I know, little human. Your little human pussy is truly mine because your little human heart is mine," he whispered. "What happened doesn't change any of that."

Her happy gaze met his, and she nuzzled his face, burrowing against his chest, her breasts happily pressing against him.

A stray look of mirth shone in Vel's gaze, though perhaps it strove to hide the sadness of their continuing captivity too.

"What is it?"

"I'm just impressed, that's all," he said, giving her forehead the caress of another kiss.

"At what?"

"You took a lot of cock, little human. A LOT. I was worried about you."

The dark humor submerged both of them like a wave and they just embraced it like two surfers, taking what the current gave them. Human and llorien, female and male, broke out in laughter.

The corrupt llorien guards had sought to break them, to break apart the bond they had together, but all it had done was make it stronger.

~ * ~

Chapter 16
Unexpected Lifeline
~ * ~ * ~ * ~

The next day they had a visitor, and it wasn't one of their corrupt guards or even their sadist prison warden. No, Unlike the guards, this llorien was dressed in immaculate red brocade. Judging from the sheen and spotlessness of the uniform, this was someone important.

"I am Kwan'rha."

Only the melodious voice and the slightly more slender stature gave the newcomer away as a female llorien.

"I have been appointed as the new warden of this prison ship. Will you please come with me?"

Kasumi and Velamar exchanged a look. The human linguist officer's raised eyebrow said it all: *She's allowing us to come with her unescorted? She's brought no guards? No protection? Either she trusts us more than I think she does, or she's got something up her sleeve in case we try anything.* Finally, Kasumi shrugged and Velamar nodded.

"Well it's not like I have anywhere else to be," Kasumi quipped. Soon, the two were following the new warden down a maze of corridors. Only when they stopped at a giant portal that snaked open from five sides at once, revealing a spacious chamber, did Kasumi realize where they'd been led. She knew because she remembered it vaguely from her first day on the ship, the day they had been 'processed' and put in shackles.

This was the warden's office.

"What happened to the previous warden?"

Kwan'rha sat down and motioned to two hovering balls (the llorien version of chairs) that sat in front of a wide zirconen surface.

"Never mind that. Please, sit." Once they had sat, Kawn'rha produced a set of heavy keys and gingerly unlocked each captive's set of shackles. She then motioned toward the far corner beside the door where they had come in. Two sets of clothes lay neatly folded there.

"Please, get dressed. I will have something brought in to eat. Would you like something to drink?"

Dumbfounded, Kasumi nodded. Velamar stared intensely at the warden with a mixture of shock and suspicion.

"You two are being... released, after a fashion. Once you sit and have put some nourishment in you, we can discuss details."

After a fashion?

Curiosity warring with her thirst and hunger, Kasumi bit her tongue only by using every ounce of willpower at her disposal. The next half hour or so was filled with the quiet sound of eating and drinking, and Kasumi and Velamar exchanging looks, trying to piece together what had happened. And all the while, Kasumi had only one thought on her mind above all others. Their own welfare be damned, she at last couldn't hold back. Not one moment longer.

"What about our child? Where is she?"

Kwan'rha nodded, her eyes dimming with surprising empathy.

"She will be allowed to join you. She will not be kept from you."

Relief flooded Kasumi. She broke down then and there. Sobs wracked her slender figure. Velamar reached out to keep her from falling. She slumped against him, clung to him, before looking back at the warden with a gaze still glistening.

"Thank you, but why? What's changed?"

"Word of your situation has reached many on our homeworld. Many llorien are outraged by the way you have been treated. It is one thing to treat a telepath harshly: after all, they are highly dangerous. But to treat a mother as you have been treated, and to separate her from her child." Kwan'rha nodded in respect toward Kasumi for all she had suffered.

"The Consul-General has seen fit to rebuke the Defense Grid Commander for his recklessness and inhumane treatment, not just of you but of all of the humans aboard the ill-fated vessel which came through the Anomaly."

"What happened to the survivors from the *Nightingale*?" Kasumi couldn't resist interrupting.

"The survivors were repatriated."

"Does this mean… will we be free to go then?"

Now Kwan'rha steepled her fingers before her.

"Not exactly."

Velamar frowned, a rumble pouring from his lips for the first time.

"Stop playing games. Please be straight with us."

"Subject 126, you and your human mate will be allowed to return to Qaephar with your child. You will be allowed to live there undisturbed. Your status as a shunned telepath and prisoner-in-exile will revert to what it was before, but you may live out your life in peace with your new interspecies family."

It wasn't everything Kasumi had been hoping for, but it was enough. Fresh tears slid down her face. Happy tears.

"Thank you." Kasumi leapt up and rushed at Kwan'rha. The surprised warden soon had a slim human wrapped around her middle, hugging her like some interstellar Santa Claus.

"You… are welcome," the warden said stiffly. Unsure what to do, unaware of the existence, let alone the purpose, of this human interpersonal custom called 'hugging,' she waited for the strange human to finish performing its arm-squeeze ritual. Finally, drawing back, Kasumi swiped at the last of her tears. She felt Vel put an arm around her shoulders. He kissed the top of her head before echoing a thanks of his own.

"You are just but also merciful, Kwan'rha. I am in your debt."

But the warden, as much as her eyes shone with pity and kindness when they looked at Kasumi, hardened as they turned toward Velamar.

"There is nothing to thank me for, Subject 126. I am merely doing my job." Kwan'rha nodded curtly toward the woman beside him. "You are fortunate to have the loyalty and devotion of a mate despite all she has had to sacrifice to be with you. See that you do not squander it or take it for granted." Now the warden stood up and four guards marched in.

"My men will escort you to the hangar. A transport is waiting. Your child will be reunited with you en route to Qaephar."

And just like that the couple's eternity of torment had ended.

~ * ~

Chapter 17
New Beginnings
~ * ~ * ~ * ~

One Week Later, On Qaephar…

The darkly-whorled grain patterns of the table in the kitchen nook shone beneath the glow-globes like the masterpiece of some artistic genius, but Velamar had only eyes for the papers splayed before him. Velamar sat there, bent over the table in study, perusing a map in his notebook, scribbling new notes to himself regarding a possible place to find new Seekstones. Although he and Kasumi had been allowed to return to Qaephar, the llorien defense grid authorities had confiscated his Seekstones. Finding more would be anything but simple.

"Any luck?" his wife called from the other room.

Kasumi had just gotten out of the shower, and she had hardly had time to dry herself, her lush cascade of ebony hair still damp. Meanwhile the baby was squalling, begging to be fed.

Little Aynira was just over six months old, but llorien babies grew much more slowly than human babies and required breastfeeding more frequently too.

The beautiful communications officer sighed. Still naked, she didn't bother taking the time to dress, instead sweeping up the child into her arms and letting the baby latch on and begin to suckle. She strode into the kitchen and wound around the corner, peering into the nook when Vel still hadn't answered.

"What's that?" Vel looked up, startled. "Sorry, dear heart. I was so absorbed. Yes, I have a few new leads. I should be able to find a new Seekstone, it will just involve venturing deeper than I have yet been. But I believe it *can* be done, and done safely."

"And do I get to join you for these excursions?" she asked with a pointed look.

"Absolutely not. Your life is too precious. Our child depends on you for nourishment."

"Oh no, buster, you aren't using that excuse on me. If we do something this important, we do it as a family. I'll strap Aynira to the front of my chest in a little parka-bag if I have to. You let me help or you don't go."

Throwing up his arms in surrender, Velamar nodded. "You are a frightening force when you are angry, little human. Did you know that?"

Kasumi's face broke out in a radiant grin that made Vel's heart leap. *I love this woman. I will always love this woman* he thought. *Sometimes the joy she gives me in just a simple look or a momentary smile takes my breath away.*

"Well, right now you can help me with the planning then. Want to sit down here? After you put the baby back down?"

The human linguist looked at her husband suspiciously. Why was there mischief in his gaze? What was he up to? She did as he asked. Once Aynira had finishing suckling from her breast, she fell asleep almost instantly when Kasumi laid her back down. Returning to the nook now, Kasumi approached cautiously, but just when she got to within arms' reach, he grabbed her around the waist and pulled her to him. Too late Kasumi realized that Velamar wasn't wearing any pants! The big alien pulled Kasumi onto his lap and sank her startled pussy onto a llorien cock that was as hard as the icy crust of Qaephar itself.

"Vel! UHHH!" Kasumi grunted as she felt her cunt absolutely stuffed. Her breasts instantly began to leak milk down her chest and onto their combined laps as arousal surged through her. Kasumi gingerly rose up and impaled herself on her alien husband's manhood.

"I can't believe we're doing this," she said with a husky hiss. "This is going to get messy."

Velamar's intense, hungry, and tender stare told her to keep going. "I can't believe your pussy hugs me so tight, woman. Don't stop for all the hemolymph on Qaephar. And you can drown me in your milk for all I care."

With her legs getting a workout, the athletic Kasumi kept going. Her body rose and fell, sucking up that purplish cock until only Velamar's testicles were visible beneath her ass cheeks. She kept riding him, his whitish-clear pre-cum combining with her own cunt juices to lubricate and make each lunge that much easier. The slippery joining of their bodies soon became a rapture that neither could deny. Even as Kasumi's supple cones leaked with a waterfall of milk, her pussy took another punishing plunge onto the hard length of llorien cock beneath her. Velamar grabbed Kasumi by the back of the head, forcing her to look him in the eye while he slipped his other hand to her too-sensitive breasts to pinch his wife's nipples with a playful grin.

"AHHH!! *Gentle*, you big ox."

"Little human, I was thinking that it might be fun to make a sibling for Aynira,"

"You don't say," Kasumi replied between groans. "Pinch my nipples again and give me a fucking baby." She leaned forward, kissing him as her cervix rested on the tip of his cock.

Moments later, as if in tacit agreement, their bodies reached climax. Kasumi moaned against Vel's lips, Kasumi's pussy clenched and convulsed with wild euphoria around Velamar's cock, and that llorien shaft lost all control. With a groan of finality, Vel exploded in her, emptying his llorien spunk deep in her fertile womb. He clamped his lips around Kasumi's nipple and drank of her milk in the throes of his release.

Little did they know it, but that night their family of three became a family of *four*.

~ * ~

Chapter 18
Reliving Versus Living
~ * ~ * ~ * ~

One Week Later…

Velamar glanced up at the mountainside as the snow-crawler drew closer.

Soon I will be back with my family. My family.

That word still struck him like a novelty, like a magical word that had no right to exist on the tip of his tongue. Yet exist it did. He had a wife and six-month-old daughter to come home to. After a day-long excursion scouring the subterranean caverns for a crystal formation like the ones which had yielded his previous three Seekstones, he had come up empty.

This may be more difficult than I thought he decided ruefully as the snow-crawler carefully ascended the last steep slope to his home carved into the mountainside, his 'Turtle's Shell' as his wife liked to call it. As he'd begun calling it too.

When he'd finished unloading the crawler and locked up the hangar, Velamar stripped out of his heavy enviro-gear and called his wife's name.

"Kasumi?"

All seemed quiet. Too quiet. Anxiety awoke. His brow knitted in worry. *Where is she?*

Their Turtle's Shell which overlooked Qaephar's wide-open ice plains was a modest series of chambers. After all, the llorien pitied their telepath outcasts enough to build some luxury into their gilded cage of a prison, but not *too* much. The entire home consisted of four chambers - a spacious bedroom, a kitchen with a small adjoining breakfast nook, a small but cozy study with a bird's eye view highest up the mountainside, and last but not least a large living area with an impressive fireplace and vaulted ceiling set with painted och'uenen timbers and mottled llorien stonework. The Turtle's Shell was a sturdy, cozy, welcoming home to return to, but it was definitely not a large space for a family of three. Sounds tended to carry, if slightly muffled, so Velamar was used to at least hearing his wife moving and always being aware of where she was. To come home now and *not* have that awareness… unsettled him.

When she didn't answer, he called again.

"Kasumi?"

With some relief, he looked at the crib set near the roaring fire in the main living chamber. Shadows danced on the vaulted ceiling like a show meant just for his daughter. The little girl lay quietly, her eyes roving back and forth, delighting in the fire's display. Her eyes brightened as her father's reassuring figure loomed above, and she squealed with delight. He picked her up and kissed her, then set her back in her crib. She resumed her fascinated staring, only this time at the fire itself instead of the shadow puppets up above.

"Where's your mother?" Velamar whispered, not expecting an answer. His cute daughter had the overall bone structure of his wife but the eyes and mottle-toned brow ridge betrayed her half-llorien ancestry. She would grow up to be a true mix of two species, and who knew: perhaps a sibling might soon join her. Velamar was hopeful.

He checked in the breakfast nook. Kasumi wasn't there. She wasn't in the bedroom either. That left only the one place she spent the least amount of time in - at least, unless he was there. Velamar's study.

Poking his head through the doorway, he realized that the smaller study fireplace had a roaring blaze going strong there too. Only the shadows cast by this fire's flickering seemed less dancing and more… brooding. Less inviting or cozy and more weighed down by some melancholy force.

He found Kasumi standing there, staring off into the flames as if every secret or puzzle she'd ever wanted answers to lay hidden somewhere in its fiery embrace.

"Kasumi?"

She turned, startled.

"Oh," she said absently. "Sorry. I didn't hear you get back."

Even a relatively oblivious and clueless male could not mistake the signs of a female this troubled.

"Kasumi, what's wrong?" *Is this why she didn't insist on joining me with Aynira in the caverns today? Why she seemed a little distant when I left?*

The Earth Alliance officer shrugged and tried to put him off. "Nothing. I'm just… tired. I should go to bed."

Now the concerned alien put both hands on her shoulders and turned her toward him. "It's not nothing. If it's nothing, then Qaephar is a desert world. Come on now. *Talk* to me."

"You don't need my burdens now," she said sadly. She looked away. A tear glistened in her eye. Then the other. Velamar cupped her face and looked at her, beseeching.

"No, give me them, woman. Stop being so stubborn." Tears filled her eyes.

"I'm a failure."

"What in the world are you talking about?" Then a gasp tore loose from his throat. He thought he knew. The epiphany struck him a sharp blow. "I know… meeting me is the worst thing that's ever happened to you. If your ship hadn't come through the Anomaly, if you hadn't ended up marooned on this planet with me… by now you would be a high-ranking officer in the Earth Alliance Fleet. An entire career, an entire future was stolen from you, Kasumi. I know this. All your ambitions, they were cruelly taken. And I am a part of that. I ask you for forgiveness that I could not do more for you. That... when the *Nightingale* tried to rescue you I could not prevent my people from-"

"No, no, no!" Kasumi blurted out, suddenly finding the strength to interrupt him. "It's not that. It's none of that." She sat down miserably on the floor before the fire and began to cry softly, softly enough so that the baby wouldn't hear.

"Then what is it?" he urged gently as he sat down beside her. He slid his arm around her shoulders and brought her close. Tucked her head beneath his chin. Kissed her soft hair which smelled like wind and rain and lilacs.

"Our daughter grew up six months without us. We've had just two weeks back with her, but I can't stop the parade of horribles that haunt my dreams. Worrying that they'll take her away from us again. That the defense grid authorities will change their minds. What will happen once the llorien people forget about us? If our case becomes less prominent? Then the defense grid can do what they want with us and revert to their old prejudices."

Kasumi stared off miserably into the flames. The crackling of the fire seemed to commisserate, the occasional hiss and pop saying '*Indeed*' or '*She is right.*'

"And even if that doesn't happen, I have other dreams. I dream of Black Diamond laughing at me. Of he and his men taking me, one after another, while you lay helpless." Kasumi turned to him, her eyes bright. "I thought I could get through this. Just throw the past behind me. It isn't that simple, though, is it?"

Vel trailed a finger tenderly down her cheek, wiping away some of her tears.

"No," he replied sadly. "It isn't." He kissed her brow and hugged her. "It will be a process. One we both must navigate." He pulled back and looked at her. "There are days when I have nightmares too.

When I dream that you and Aynira will be taken from me, dooming me to live utterly lost and alone."

Kasumi cupped his cheek even as he cupped hers. Her fingers seemed to stroke the skin there as if she wanted to memorize every contour, every curve.

"What are we going to do? This is… this is no way to live."

"This isn't living, Kas. This is *reliving*. We are reliving our trauma and letting it project onto the present and into our future. That is no way to live. It is understandable. It is even normal for those who have been through all we have been through. But it cannot *become* our new normal. We must overcome it. We cannot let it take us down the path of darkness and despair."

Now the black-haired human shook her head sadly, chuckling with little mirth.

"Yes, but how? How do we overcome it?" She threw an attempt at humor at him. "Do you know a good therapist on Qaephar? Maybe one of those snow beetles could listen to my cares."

Velamar pulled Kasumi against him again, kissing the top of her head and giving her a loving squeeze. "I do not, little human. But I do know this: there are many reasons to have hope. We are together. That is something. Our family is strong if we lean on each other and look out for each other. I see the way you look at little Aynira. The very sight of her gives you joy and purpose. I see it." He smiled down at her and kissed her on the lips. "That little being, that little beautiful miracle of a life we created, will help us get through this." Velamar paused, seeing that he'd breathed some hope into his wife as she looked back at him.

"I do have some good news to report as well. I meant to tell you yesterday when we received our latest supply shipment, but I got too distracted with logistics for my cave-diving Seekstone expedition."

"Speaking of which, how did that go? Any luck?" Kasumi asked.

"Not yet. But let me finish." He placed a fingertip to her lips to shush her and smiled. "We received a message from Kwan'rha. Seems that she has taken a very personal interest in our case. In her message she said that if we ever need any medical care, to use this emergency device." Velamar pulled out a small oblong instrument with a short antennae. "This transmitter, when activated, will alert her. She will give us access to her ship's best doctors if we ever have need."

Kasumi smiled for the first time in a while, a ray of sunshine through too many clouds.

"So someone still cares up there," Kasumi marveled. "It was more than I was willing to hope for."

"Indeed," Velamar replied, and before he could say anything more Kasumi leaned forward and kissed him. Her lips melted against his, but then her hungry tongue slipped past his defenses, eager, passionate, and loving.

"You're good at this, you know."

"Good at what?" he asked, stroking her hair, basking in the glory of his wife's beautiful face.

"Reassuring me. Knowing what I need to hear sometimes."

"Well I only do so because I am the luckiest male this side of the Morclunaxian Galaxy."

Kasumi arched an eyebrow. "Oh really? Only *this side*?" she teased.

He laughed and so did she. Their laughter intertwined like the double helix of DNA, creating a perfect union, a symmetry brimming with a love that would never die.

~ * ~

The past was not yet behind Velamar or Kasumi. No past ever truly is. The trauma from their time on the prison ship would take years to heal from, would take years to soften like jagged glass made smooth and forgiving by the patience of the sea. But that day would come, and in the meantime they would have two little bundles of life to fill their days and overflow their hearts. Little Aynira and her brother Camruu would grow to be kind and loving, strong and fearless. They would become a credit to their parents, to an inter-species couple who had made a life for themselves even in the midst of a bleak world of jagged cliffs and treacherous ice.

To the llorien authorities Qaephar was an icy, desolate hellscape of a planet. But to Kasumi and Velamar it was something else. *Home.*

~ * ~

THE END

~ * ~

About Dakota Kaine
~ * ~

Dakota Kaine likes to write about strong but vulnerable heroines and the sexy aliens who love them. A traveler at heart, Dakota adores the stuff of romance whenever going abroad - whether that be castles (Dakota has been to dozens of them!) or the picturesque vineyards of Germany and Italy. If you enjoyed this book, feel free to email Dakota at: **Dakotakaine103@gmail.com**

Author's Note
~ * ~

Thank you for reading *Kasumi and The Alien.* In writing this book I was hoping to combine erotica with a meaningful story and relationship at its core. In Kasumi and Velamar, I hope I have done that goal justice. The world is a judgemental place and while some of the sexual scenes in this book may seem 'out there' and especially vivid, I would argue that there is a healthy exploration of fantasies that erotica fosters, one that I think is far healthier than the more socially acceptable interests strewn throughout our society. As a society we elevate violence and other brutal pastimes but then clutch our pearls when sex is celebrated or depicted too openly. In its own small way, *Kasumi and the Alien* is a push against that. *Kasumi and the Alien* is hopefully a reminder to you, if you are reading this, that exploring sexual fantasies through the written word isn't shameful - it's a magical part of what it means to be human.

Made in the USA
Las Vegas, NV
04 March 2026

43057235R00076